SHIPMENT FIVE

Belonging to Bandera by Tina Leonard
Court Me, Cowboy by Barbara White Daille
His Best Friend's Bride by Jodi O'Donnell
The Cowboy's Return by Linda Warren
Baby Be Mine by Victoria Pade
The Cattle Baron by Margaret Way

SHIPMENT SIX

Crockett's Seduction by Tina Leonard
Coming Home to the Cattleman by Judy Christenberry
Almost Perfect by Judy Duarte
Cowboy Dad by Cathy McDavid
Real Cowboys by Roz Denny Fox
The Rancher Wore Suits by Rita Herron
Falling for the Texas Tycoon by Karen Rose Smith

SHIPMENT SEVEN

Last's Temptation by Tina Leonard
Daddy by Choice by Marin Thomas
The Cowboy, the Baby and the Bride-to-Be by Cara Colter
Luke's Proposal by Lois Faye Dyer
The Truth About Cowboys by Margot Early
The Other Side of Paradise by Laurie Paige

SHIPMENT EIGHT

Mason's Marriage by Tina Leonard
Bride at Briar's Ridge by Margaret Way
Texas Bluff by Linda Warren
Cupid and the Cowboy by Carol Finch
The Horseman's Son by Delores Fossen
Cattleman's Bride-to-Be by Lois Faye Dyer

The rugged, masculine and independent men
of America's West know the value of hard work,
honor and family. They may be ranchers, tycoons
or the guy next door, but they are all cowboys at heart.
Don't miss any of the books in this collection!

Cowboy
at
Heart

HIS BEST FRIEND'S BRIDE
JODI
O'DONNELL

USA TODAY Bestselling Author

HARLEQUIN® COWBOY AT HEART

Recycling programs
for this product may
not exist in your area.

ISBN-13: 978-0-373-82628-5

HIS BEST FRIEND'S BRIDE

Printed in U.S.A.

www.Harlequin.com

JODI O'DONNELL

grew up one of fourteen children in small-town Iowa. As a result, she loves to explore in her writing how family relationships influence who and why we love as we do.

A *USA TODAY* bestselling author, Jodi has also been a finalist for Romance Writers of America's RITA® Award and is a past winner of RWA's Golden Heart Award. She lives in Iowa.

To Diane Grecco:
thanks for your hard work and enthusiasm—
you made my first series a wonderful experience!

Prologue

A maternity ward in south central Texas, 26 years ago.

"What a darling face she has."

At the pronouncement, Mary Jo Sennett turned to find a young woman about her age standing next to her and gazing through the plate-glass window at the rows of newborns on the other side that were lined up like crates of fresh produce.

"That's your daughter, isn't it, the third one from the left in the first row?" the other woman responded to Mary Jo's quizzical look. "What a crop of blond hair she has, too! Like a perfect angel. I'm afraid my baby's hair is going to be like mine—black as coal and unruly as a horse's tail."

With a comical expression, she grabbed a handful of her curly hair, which was indeed an unusually deep black, as if to pull it out by the roots, making Mary Jo laugh, then wince.

"Ow!" She rubbed her sore tummy muscles through her robe. "Well, she may look like a perfect angel in that bassinet, but on her way to bein' born she was more like the Tasmanian devil."

Now the other woman laughed, a pearly peal down the scale, like someone playing a xylophone. "Sounds like you've got a live one on your hands."

Mary Jo decided she liked this woman, with her curly black hair and musical laugh. She and her husband Andy were new to this part of Texas, having only recently moved to Bridgewater, a little-dot-on-the-map-size town eighty miles or so west of the Houston metro area. Andy was a lineman for the power company—just like in the Glen Campbell song, they often joked—and the move would be a good one for the family…eventually. Right now, though, Mary Jo was homesick for her old house, her old street and her old neighbors, most of all.

She stared at the other mother with what she was greatly afraid bordered on longing. This was a regional hospital. Not much hope that this woman and her family would hail from Bridgewater, too, given the vast area and number of small towns served by the facility.

Well, she thought philosophically, at least the two of them could be friends for as long as they were here. Of course, she didn't even know her name, but they already had babies who shared the same birth date. Many a friendship had started on less.

Mary Jo obligingly peered through the glass and spotted an infant with a cap of the thickest, blackest hair she'd ever seen on a baby. "So I'm guessing the one on my daughter's right is yours?"

"That's my boy," she answered as she gazed at the newborn with loving eyes. "The first of many children, we hope."

Mary Jo beamed at her child, as well. "Julia's my second, although my first girl."

Intelligent blue eyes glanced across at her. "Is that the name you've chosen? Julia?"

"Yes. Julia Marie. What have you decided to name yours?"

The other woman wrinkled her nose attractively. "Oh, we haven't settled on it yet. Isn't that terrible? It's not like we haven't had nine whole months to mull it over."

"Something'll come to you, you'll see,"

Mary Jo assured her. "Something just perfect for him."

They stood in companionable silence for a long moment, watching their babies make the funny faces babies do, smacking their lips and popping their eyes open, only to screw them closed a moment later.

"They look like a little bride and groom, don't you think?" the other woman said out of the blue.

Mary Jo smiled at the whimsicalness of the notion, but knew exactly the impression from which it sprang. "You mean, how their bassinets are lined up side by side, and she's so blond and he's got such black hair—"

"It's like they're two seconds from saying their 'I do's,'" the other mother finished gaily, then pointed. "Oops! Except here comes some scoundrel to break them up."

Sure enough, a nurse was moving the little black-haired infant aside and inserting another bassinet between the two babies.

Mary Jo affected dismay, theatrically pressing her palms to her cheeks. "Oh, no! What kind of dastardly villain would come between true love?"

"That would be my dastardly villain," came a cheerful voice from behind them.

Mary Jo and her companion turned. Sitting in a wheelchair to one side was another young woman, obviously a new mother like themselves, smiling in a way that could only be described as roguish.

She wheeled herself forward. "Of course, I'd hate to think my son has sealed his fate as a blackguard just for throwin' his hat into the ring, so to speak."

Mary Jo and her friend both spoke at once. "Oh, heavens, no!"

"We were only joking!"

They each took a step toward the other mother as she caught hold of the handrail along the wall and struggled to stand.

"Here, let me help you," Mary Jo said, taking her under the elbow.

"Oh, thanks. I should be in bed—the baby just wasn't comin' along, and my doctor had to do a cesarean, y'see—but I had to sneak a peek at my little one."

"I'm sure he's worth every bit of difficulty," Mary Jo said.

The woman looked up at her gratefully, and that's when Mary Jo noticed that she, too, had pitch-black hair, although hers was long and straight.

How strange, Mary Jo thought, to meet two

women—and new mothers such as herself—with hair of such an unusual shade. But then really, what was so remarkable? After all, she *was* standing in a maternity ward!

Steadying herself with their support, the newest addition to their group gave a sigh as all three lost themselves in contemplation of the new lives they'd created.

"I can't wait for my mother to get here," Mary Jo's first acquaintance spoke up. "My husband drove back to Bridgewater to pick her up."

"You live in Bridgewater?" Mary Jo exclaimed, staring at her. "I just moved there! We bought a house on Chestnut Street."

"No! Chestnut? That's just one street over from Oak, where I live."

The mother on her other side gaped at the two of them. "This is so strange. *I* live on Oak, between Fourth and Fifth streets. We haven't lived there long—just bought the house from my in-laws."

There was a stupefied silence, then all three women began chattering at once. "This is amazing!" "What are the chances, do you think?" "We've got to get together, all our families!" "What if our babies became best friends for life?" "We don't even know each others' names, for heaven's sake!"

They were distracted from exchanging those names, though, when both Mary Jo's and the first of her new friend's babies started to fuss, then to cry, then to cry even harder, tiny fists waving in the air.

"Uh-oh, this could put a kink in our plans," Mary Jo joked. "I don't think those two are gonna like another man coming between them."

Linking arms, the women laughed. Now *that* was just too absurd. After all, they were just three little babies, with their personalities yet to be determined, their lives and fates yet to be written.

Chapter One

Griff Corbin cracked open a can of Coke, leaned one hip against the side of the worn wooden counter inside Kearney's Tack and Feed, and took a long, leisurely swallow as he settled in for a wait.

Dale Kearney, on the business side of the counter, had just received a phone call of sparse interaction consisting mainly of "'Lo, Kearney's…a-yup… nope…he shore 'nough is…I'll tell him…you bet," all the while gazing at his sole patron with that expressionless gaze that reminded Griff of nothing so much as a steer chewing its cud.

Dale had hung up and informed him, "That schoolteacher friend of yours is on her way over. Some kind of emergency. Said it was important."

Lifting his faded gimme cap, this one from a supplier of a feed supplement, he scratched his balding head with supreme disinterest, tugged it back on and said, "I'll be out back unloadin' a shipment of salt blocks if ya got a question. Or just leave a note what you took and I'll bill ya like usual."

His own curiosity only slightly more piqued, Griff decided to make use of his unscheduled break to take a stab at guessing what "that schoolteacher friend" had on her mind this time. The last situation Julia Sennett had deemed a dire emergency was when she'd heard Skip Goslin, the postmaster, had decided to start shooting the crows that roosted in the pecan trees outside the post office after Esther Biddle complained of being dive-bombed by one and having her new hat destroyed.

Griff had listened patiently as Julia had gone on about cruelty to animals and all that, pointing out that the crows *were* a local nuisance. Although, in Griff's technical opinion, so were Esther's hats. In the end, he'd helped Julia to put an awning above the walkway to the post office, thereby saving not only populations of crows and hats, but the heads and shoulders of every postal patron, as well.

That was Julia for you. She'd always been a champion for animals, as well as the young, the old, the infirm and the unfortunate. She'd been that way all of her life—and he'd known her for the main of it.

He took another hefty swig of Coke. Part of the reason Julia was the way she was, he guessed, was because she'd lost her mother when only five and had been raised by her older brother, Ty, and her father, Andy. And while she might be a schoolteacher, she was unlike any he'd ever known. She'd gone off with the Peace Corps out of college and worked in Central America, then come back and gotten hired on to teach second grade at the elementary school in town, and was, by golly, making the administrators wonder what kind of wildcat they'd taken on.

Yep, Julia was game for anything, it had always seemed. As was Reb. And he, himself, until that encounter with an ornery cuss of a bull had given him something to think about, meaning his own mortality.

Griff cocked his head at the sound of squealing tires. That would be her now. Through Kearney's plate-glass window he saw a blue SUV pull up to the curb. Out jumped a woman dressed in a pair of khaki slacks and a fleece vest the exact shade of pale green to set off her blond good looks to a T.

She yanked open the door, and the way her gaze frantically searched the interior gave Griff his first inkling that something really serious was about to go down.

Setting aside his Coke, he pushed himself off from the counter and started toward her. He'd taken only a step when her eyes homed in on him and filled with such relief, such need, that he experienced the twinge of an emotion he thought he'd successfully freeze-dried, vacuum-sealed and stored in the most remote recesses of his heart years ago.

It came to life instantly, though—like a seed germinating and sprouting to maturity in the space of a second—when Julia Sennett, his best friend in the whole world, threw herself at him and clung to him like a vine.

On reflex, Griff wrapped his arms around her, barely believing that this woman, whom he'd have bet the ranch had never experienced a moment of fear or doubt in her life, was nearly trembling with both.

His eyes closed automatically to savor this once-in-a-lifetime feeling.

"What is it, Julia?" he asked into her hair. "What's wrong?"

"Oh, Griff!" She flung back her head, her arms still locked around his neck so that their faces were a mere inch apart. Tears sparkled in those multifaceted hazel eyes of hers that had always reminded him, unlikely as it seemed, of a grove of oak trees at dawn, leaves rustling in the breeze.

"What is it, darlin'?" he murmured. "You can tell me."

"It…it's Reb," she answered, her lips quivering. "He's written to say he's having second thoughts about marrying me. Why? Why wouldn't he want to marry me?"

JULIA WATCHED GRIFF'S violet-blue eyes widen in surprise, then narrow in a manner she'd never before witnessed. She'd have to be blind not to get their meaning, which sure enough came through loud and clear: *danger ahead.*

"Griff, no," she said hastily. "I didn't tell you so you could go and get all mad at Reb, which I can see from your face that you are."

"Then what *did* you tell me for?" he asked with deadly calm.

"For help, of course! I only want to understand—understand what might be going through Reb's mind that he'd think maybe the two of us weren't meant for each other."

"And I'm supposed to help you how?" he said quietly, setting her already-stirred-up apprehensions churning.

Of course, Griff had always been the calm, cool and collected one of the three friends. It was something she'd come to count on. But this kind of calm was unnerving.

"How can you help me?" she echoed. "Aside from myself, no one knows Reb, inside and out, better than you, that's how!"

Seeking reassurance, she gazed desperately up at those familiar features she knew as well as her own: the wide forehead over which his soot-black hair was always falling, his strong jaw perennially silhouetted by the five o'clock shadow of as dark a beard. Those eyes of such a feminine shade of violet blue that she'd teased him unmercifully nearly from the moment she could form the words.

The three of them—herself, Griff and Reb Farley—had been friends since birth, the bond between them as inviolable as blood relation, the love between them as unconditional. Which also meant they knew each other's faults all too well. And if Reb had both a shortcoming and an attribute, it was his single-mindedness when it came to going after what he wanted. It was what had just recently made him a world champion bull rider.

It was also what had earned him her promise to marry him more than a year ago. But he'd wanted to get that golden belt buckle before setting the wedding date. They'd intended to do that when he came home this time.

Now, though, they might not do anything of the sort.

That was why she couldn't deny it: deep down, Julia was just a mite gratified by Griff's obvious and rare anger on her behalf. Yet there was that something else she saw in his gaze. Something just as out-of-the-ordinary.

Or something, actually, that she hadn't seen in a long, long time.

She realized they still stood locked in each other's arms in a lover-like embrace. It dawned on her at the same time that at some point Dale Kearney had wandered to the front of his store and was now looking on in extreme curiosity—or with as much curiosity as someone whose usual expression was that of a stone slab could exhibit.

Griff seemed to come to the same realization just as she did. He released his hold on her waist as Julia slid her arms from around his neck. They each took an awkward step backward.

"Say, Dale…" Griff said, giving a discreet cough and a not-very-subtle nod in her direction. "I know this is your place of business and all, but it doesn't look like this is your rush hour. Would you mind finding something to keep you occupied so we can have some privacy?"

Dale stood rooted to his spot for the longest five seconds of Julia's life. Then, bless him, he shrugged and headed off in the direction of his office.

Griff watched him go before turning back to her. "Now, why don't you fill me in on just what sort of second thoughts Reb's having that could possibly give you the impression he wants to call off your wedding."

"I got this letter from him this morning," she explained, pulling the folded envelope from her slacks' pocket. She almost handed it to Griff before remembering the private nature of its contents. "I'd just finished up my classes and had sat down to read it at my desk. It says he's coming home at Christmas for the big celebration the town's getting up for him on New Year's Eve, on account of his winning the championship in Las Vegas last week. He's even plannin' on staying a week or two so he can spend time with the two of us before he heads to the Fort Worth Stock Show."

Grasping the envelope in both hands, she held the letter in front of her as if taking its measure. How could so light and thin a parcel contain such stunning news? "But he says he's had some time to think while he's been on the road. And he wondered if we ought to take a step back before setting a date for the wedding."

The news hit her afresh and Julia glanced up at Griff helplessly, more at a loss for what to do than she'd ever been in her life. "It's just so out-of-the-blue. What could have happened to change his feelings for me?"

Griff said nothing, but the quiet intensity that reminded her of a storm ready to cut loose at any second returned to his eyes, confusing her again. The reaction was simply not the characteristic of the man she knew. If anything, he'd always been nearly the exact opposite: *nothing* had the power to get his dander up. Easygoing to a fault, she'd never in her life seen him truly angry—or show any other strong emotion, for that matter.

Not that he was of Dale Kearney's stone-faced ilk. Griff could be funny, teasing, annoyed, sad or affectionate, as the situation warranted. But she'd often wondered what it would take to roust him out of his complacency.

Well, this just might be the acid test, she realized as he asked, "Does Reb give any clues at all as to the nature of his doubts?" He paused. "I don't know, like…there's someone else?"

At his question, Julia felt her own ire hit a new high.

"There'd better not be anyone else!" she declared. "I mean, I know there're dozens of buckle bunnies at every stop on the circuit who'd love to lasso themselves a rodeo star, but Reb always said he'd as soon wrestle a rattlesnake as get caught in one of their traps."

Yet *could* that be what the problem was? Julia wondered. The mere prospect that it might be devastated her. She stared at the diamond solitaire on her left hand as if it were an oracle. If Reb had had doubts about the two of them making a life together that had led him to a dalliance, or if he truly *had* fallen for another woman, he owed it to her to tell her flat-out.

Or did Griff already know that this was what this Dear Jane letter was about, and Reb was counting on him to break the news in person?

At the thought, she gaped at him in hurt. "Do you *know* if there's someone else, Griff?" Surprise leapt to his eyes, making Julia's heart squeeze in real pain. "If you do, why didn't you tell me? Who could have come between us?"

Not answering, Griff pivoted away from her to stare out the window, taking a few steps with that hitched gait of his that was so much a part of him now it barely registered on her mind—except for that arrow of empathy, its sharpness dulled with use, that invariably besieged her heart.

Gaze trained out the window, he asked with sudden gentleness, "What if there was... someone else? What would you do?"

She shook her head in confusion. "I don't know!" It simply didn't seem like Reb. She knew he loved her.

But she also knew that he had a...a burning desire within him to win at whatever he did—even at the cost of those around him. How that need might have manifested itself in this situation, she couldn't have said for the world. But ever since she'd read his letter, she'd had a glimmering that it was connected to that issue.

"I don't know what I'd do," she repeated, gripping her elbows with her opposite hands. "I'd be pretty angry with him for being dishonest and disloyal."

"And friends don't treat friends that way," Griff added almost to himself.

"Exactly. So do you…know something I don't?" she asked him. "Because if there *is* someone else, that's a deal-breaker, as far as I'm concerned. Anything else I can handle."

He turned his head and looked at her, and she had the strangest impression that it was on the tip of his tongue to reveal some secret he'd been holding inside for a long, long time.

It raised the fine hairs on the back of her neck.

"You better tell me if you know, Griff Corbin, and none of that we-cowboys-gotta-stick-together stuff that you and Reb always pull on me!" she declared.

Perversely, that brought the sliver of a smile to his mouth and a hint of the Griff she knew to his violet-blue eyes. "Be fair, Julia. We haven't done that since you tattled to our mamas 'bout how we roped Mrs. White's mailbox and accidentally tore the post out of the ground when Reb's horse got spooked and lit for the highway."

"I didn't tattle. Both your mothers knew darn well you were responsible. They only asked me to confirm it, and I wasn't about to lie to them."

"And you wouldn't lie to anyone, would you, Julia? Most of all yourself?" he asked with that strange quietness.

"Of course not!" Julia said, more confused than ever.

His chin dropped and he contemplated the worn wooden floor for a few moments as she waited on tenterhooks. Finally he said, "There's no one else, Julia. Not that I know of. Anyway, that kind of thing doesn't sound like Reb."

Her shoulders slumped in relief.

"So what do I do, Griff?" She paced to one end of the counter, turned and paced to the other end. "I'd call him if I only knew where he was stayin'—or in what town. But you know Reb. He'll pick up the phone when he's got a free moment. He does say in his letter we'll talk about the matter more when he comes home over Christmas."

She stopped dead in her tracks in front of

him, her jaw dropping in horror. "Good heavens, I just remembered! A bunch of people are supposed to meet tonight so we can organize Reb's big homecoming celebration! And I'm in charge! How am I going tell them Reb and I might not be getting married?"

He still looked at her with that expression whose meaning she wasn't sure of though it raised all kinds of apprehensions in her that somehow, some way, the chance existed that she'd lose him, too.

It was just too staggering to conceive, and her eyes filled with tears again. "Griff, you know how it's been for me. I've always counted on two certainties in my life—my family, Daddy and Ty, and my two closest, dearest friends in the world, you and Reb. And now one of those friends, for all intents and purposes might be quitting me! It doesn't seem possible."

She stared up at him, fighting back the strongest urge to throw herself once more into his comforting embrace. "It's just that, you—you're my best friend. You've always been there for me, through thick and thin. And ever since I walked in here, I've had the most awful feeling you know somethin' I don't—or that you're getting set to quit me, too."

At her words, his expression finally softened and changed back to the one she'd grown up knowing.

"That could never happen," he said with conviction. He lifted his hand as if to touch her face, and she remembered the tenderness in his voice as he'd asked her what was wrong—and how he could fix it. For that moment, she had felt as if she could have handled anything, every doubt on Reb's part, with Griff beside her.

She felt that way now—until his arm fell back to his side.

"You want to know what to do?" he said. "Well, here's the deal, Julia. You're still gonna plan that celebration just like you intended. I'll help, every step of the way, do whatever you need me to do. And we won't tell anyone Reb's having second thoughts."

"N-not tell anyone?" she stammered, those feelings of security deserting her, especially when he set his jaw. "But what if he comes back and we can't work it out?"

She'd never seen her friend look so grim or as grimly resolved.

"Then we'll deal with that if and when it happens. But for now, as far as anyone's concerned," he continued with emphasis, "as far as you are—as far as I am—you're still gonna get married, just you wait and see."

Julia blinked. "How can you know that for sure?"

GRIFF STEELED HIMSELF against the confused uncertainty in her hazel eyes that he knew he could easily use to turn her favor toward him—and away from Reb.

Friends didn't do that to friends, however. She trusted him implicitly; that was why she'd come to him for help. And he was Reb's friend as much as he was Julia's. He didn't know at this point what Reb's reasons were for sending her such a letter. But Griff knew his friend well enough to know there *was* some reason, and if he felt it best to make his explanations in person, then Julia should trust that Reb had her best interests at heart.

As for himself, Griff knew Reb's explanation better be solid sterling, or his friend would have hell to pay.

"You were right—I *do* know Reb as well as I know you," he told her. "As well as I know myself. And whatever his doubts, they're not because he doesn't care for you anymore."

He noted the whisper of comfort that whisked across her face at that assertion, which only strengthened his resolve to get Julia and Reb through this rough patch.

"We owe him the benefit of the doubt," Griff went on more firmly. "We—you, I mean—owe him time to think on the matter some more, so that when he comes home, the two of you can talk it through like couples do when they hit snags in their relationships, and work out whatever doubts he's got."

He smiled in what he hoped was a wry way but was afraid was more cynical than anything. "After all, Reb may be the world champion at bull riding, but he can be goosey as any cowboy when it comes to a woman."

Her hazel eyes flashed up at him. "But I'm not some...some *woman*. This is me!"

The hurt bewilderment in her voice ripped into him. It was durn difficult trying to keep himself from working up a good mad at his friend, even harder not to take her into his arms to comfort her in the way she deserved to be, in the way he so wanted to— had wanted to all his life.

But he couldn't. If he had to go away again to keep himself from doing so, he would.

"And it's Reb. You *know* how he can be." He had to be frank with her, but he walked the finest of lines here. "He's always had that side to him, where he'd step into a situation before he'd had a chance to think about all the what-ifs. I've always thought it was havin' that quality that's made him a top-notch bull rider. You've got to risk losin' to win, and the bigger the stakes, the bigger both the risk and the reward."

And I've lost at that game. The thought made Griff grind his molars.

"So you think he rushed into asking me to marry him, and *that's* why he's having second thoughts? Or he feels I rushed him?" Her mouth worked as she tried to understand. "But it was almost a year before I said yes! How is that rushing into anything?"

"I didn't mean either of you rushed," Griff said hastily, wondering madly how he could give her what she needed right now. "I only meant it was natural for him to be searchin' right now, and you gotta give him time to work things through."

He took her by her upper arms. "Think about it. Reb finally won the world championship in bull riding that he's been yearnin' for since we were all knee high to a fence post, and he's realizing he's accomplished one of his biggest life goals long before he's even thirty."

Unlike yourself, his inner voice taunted.

He ignored it while watching as she processed what he'd said. He hoped to God he'd been convincing, although he had no assurance of that. He was simply too close to the matter. Too close to both of these people who meant the world to him.

"So you think this is just a phase, Griff?" she finally asked.

He experienced a measure of triumph that almost checked the yearning for a much different outcome. For while the chances of achieving his most cherished of dreams had improved incrementally with today's developments, he still didn't hold out a lot of hope that his dream would come true.

"Yeah, cut him some slack," he said with conviction. "Wait till he gets back to town, show him how much he…he means to you—" his voice cracked traitorously "—and he'll realize how much you mean to him."

Her hazel eyes were huge. "You really think so?"

"I guarantee it."

Her sigh of relief was palpable. "All right. We'll wait and see." She smiled up at him in complete trust. "Thank you, Griff. I knew you'd know what to do."

He shrugged off her compliment, but was glad she couldn't see his face when she gave him another of her spontaneous, friendly hugs, as guilt reared its ugly head within him.

The next couple of weeks were going to be the most difficult of his entire life. Being gored by a bull was a piece of cake in comparison.

Because Griff knew that, really, if he was anywhere close to being noble about this whole matter, it was because deep down he still nourished the faintest hope that Julia and Reb *would* break it off for good.

And if they did, his only chance of eventually winning her himself would depend upon his being scrupulously upright in his intentions throughout her time of need.

Chapter Two

Griff entered the home he'd grown up in to the scent of warm apple pie and the sound of his mother softly singing George Strait's "Check Yes or No" as she puttered in the kitchen.

He wasn't sure what kind of sign he considered it that the song was about two people who meet as children and fall in love for keeps.

As he shed his sheepskin jacket and hung his Stetson on a peg in the back porch, he managed to paste on his usual end-of-the-workday look of interest in what was for dinner before stepping into the kitchen.

"That sure smells good," he said for emphasis.

Frannie Corbin turned and smiled at her son. "I used the first of the apples I put up for the winter," she informed him. "The nip in the air made it feel so much like Christmas was really coming, I just had to."

"And you wouldn't believe me when I told you they hadn't knocked the holiday off the calendar this year, much as you fretted."

His mother cast him a tolerant glance. "I only said I was findin' it hard to get into the Christmas mood, that's all."

Griff dropped a kiss on his mother's cheek as he passed by on his way to the fridge. Actually, he was glad she was feeling more excited. It had been tough for her—tough for them both—since Web Corbin had died fourteen months ago. Griff had been living and working in the Panhandle—his last-ditch attempt to put a certain situation out of his mind—but had immediately moved back to Bridgewater to be with his mother.

He wasn't a bit sorry to have returned, would do it again in a flash. Frannie often said the good Lord never gave anyone more than they could handle. Griff just wished his Maker didn't have quite so much confidence in him.

"Well, if you're itchin' to dig out your decorations and lights and put 'em up, you don't have to go over to the church hall for that meeting tonight." He cleared his throat.

"You know, to plan Reb's homecoming celebration."

Frannie paused in her task of slicing tomatoes for the salad to look at him quizzically. "Of course I'm going to the meeting! I told Andy Sennett I'd be there. We were talkin' after square dancing the other night, and he's thinkin' he'd like some kind of theme for the celebration for his future son-in-law."

Griff merely lifted his eyebrows as he dipped into the fridge and pulled out a Lonestar. He had often wondered about the exact nature of his mother's relationship with Julia's father. Andy had never married after losing his wife those years ago, and since the death of Griff's father, Frannie and Andy had found a lot of comfort in each other's friendship.

Of course, the two of them probably didn't know themselves the exact nature of that friendship, or at least weren't about to act upon any wayward feelings of romance that might crop up now and again.

There must be something in the town's water, Griff decided, that made its inhabitants so durned fainthearted at love.

"We were thinking of something like 'The bull stops here,'" Frannie went on blithely. "Or maybe 'Reb-el with a cause.'"

She straightened as if poked in the spine with a cattle prod. "Or I know! 'Golden buckles—and wedding bands'!"

Griff hid a wince under cover of twisting the cap off his beer bottle, from which he then took a welcome draft.

"What I actually meant," he said, leaning against the counter, "was that I'd be goin' to the meetings and helping out with planning Reb's party. So I'll be able to represent the family on the committee. I don't think both Corbins need to be workin' their fingers to the bone on this shindig."

Griff couldn't keep the slightest hint of resentfulness out of his voice, and he damned himself for it.

Especially when his mother leveled one of her most probing looks at him, joined eyebrows and all.

His only chance was to take the offensive. "Oh, don't be givin' me the hairy eyeball," he said. "You'll have plenty of chances to put your fingerprint on this celebration—literally. After that cake you made for Aunt Pauline and Uncle Dooley's ceremony to renew their weddin' vows, nobody's gonna even try their hand at one for Reb."

Tipping back his head, he took another

greatly needed swig of beer before adding, "It's just that Julia asked me to sit on the committee as a special favor to her and Reb. After all, they're my two best friends."

Frannie continued to study him as if he were a bug under a microscope. Finally she said, "Well, if that's what Julia wants. She knows Reb's wishes just about as well as anyone."

"You'd think," Griff muttered as his mother went on with making a salad, the matter apparently settled. He breathed a silent sigh of relief. He did not want his mother at that meeting tonight, and that was the short and long of it. She had some of the best powers of intuition this side of the Brazos, and it would take her about two minutes to spot the tension in Julia—and the tension in him while around her.

He helped his mother put the rest of dinner on the table, as was their routine. They ate with a minimum of fuss, exchanging stories on the events of their day and sharing the concerns in their lives, and Griff thought he'd successfully put her off the scent for good.

Until Frannie pushed her dessert plate aside, set her elbows on the table and asked bluntly, "So what's goin' on?"

"Goin' on?" he parroted inanely, almost choking on his last bite of apple pie.

"I know you and Reb love each other like brothers, but even brothers have their differences." Her eyes were knowing. "Their competitiveness with each other."

"I don't know what you mean," Griff said somewhat primly, trying to keep his stomach from careering around his body like a Mexican jumping bean.

Frannie sighed. "You don't say it, Griff, don't show it either, to your credit. But it's got to be hard on you watchin' Reb make all the dreams you once had come true by winnin' that championship."

So *that* was what she meant. Griff almost smiled. "I don't regret havin' to give up rodeoing after my accident, Mom. I honestly don't. You and Dad always taught me that things happen for a reason, and it seems my path in life wasn't about ridin' broncs or bulls."

"For which I'm eternally grateful, as a mother. But I would've supported you in that calling, if it was what you wanted."

"It might've been at one time, but not anymore." He leaned his chair back on two legs in contemplation. "If anything, I think havin' a limitation like I did was good for me—made me develop other skills and talents."

Frannie's expression was tender as she regarded him. "Well, I know you're never happier than when you're riding through a herd of cattle, checking them over."

"I *am* happy managing Tanglewood for Connor Brody. He's a great boss to have. And a great friend," he said, meaning it.

"And just think, if your dad's death hadn't brought you back to Bridgewater, you wouldn't have taken on the foreman's job at Tanglewood, and you would never have suggested your cousin for the physician's assistant position at the clinic, and Connor and Lara would never have met and fallen in love."

She shook her head, marveling. "Makes you wonder what's in store for you just around that turn in road, doesn't it?"

"It sure does," Griff agreed, but without quite the trustful sentiment. The front legs of his chair dropped to the floor with a *thunk*. "Well, let me help you get the kitchen cleaned up before I head over to the meeting."

Mother and son worked companionably, and it wasn't long before Frannie hied herself up to the attic to locate her boxes of Christmas decorations, along with her promise to call Griff when she needed a hand hauling them downstairs. In the meantime, he grabbed another beer and took it out onto the front porch with him.

There surely was a nip in the air that was a harbinger of Christmas, although the holiday in south central Texas was no snowy affair, not by a long shot. But the nights would turn more chilly, and everyone would pretend that it was cold enough to indulge in such time-honored holiday activities as sipping hot cocoa and snuggling in front of a fire with the one you loved most…

Griff scowled. Truly, on the whole he was quite content with his lot in life. He found his work fulfilling, found the fellowship he had with his friends and family satisfying. He'd never been one to waste much time on what might have been, because as his mother had aptly pointed out, things did happen for a reason.

And clearly, he wasn't meant to be with Julia Sennett.

He stared up at the night sky, his thoughts going back over a decade, despite himself. Of course, it wasn't as if he'd ever forget that day when they all—Julia, Reb and himself—had been a few months past fifteen years old.

They'd grown up learning to rope and ride beside each other. And up till they were about ten, the three of them had kept pace with each other. After that point, though, the boys had pulled slowly away from Julia in strength and agility—and sheer reckless energy.

That was when things had started to turn competitive between him and Reb, for the first time in their friendship. His mother had the right of it there. The two of them were well matched when it came to most cowboy skills, but it had become clear to just about anyone who watched them practice that riding broncs was a skill Griff had over Reb in spades. While Griff had been raised better than to throw his superior skills in his friend's face, the comparison had been unavoidable, given how much time they spent in each other's company…along with Julia.

Yes, then there was the matter of Julia.

Griff closed his eyes and permitted himself an exploratory ramble into emotional territory from which he'd banned himself long ago. Even at fifteen she'd been a beauty, with that long, honey-colored hair and startlingly clear hazel eyes fringed by dark gold lashes.

That had only been part of her fascination, however. She was passionate about…oh, everything, it seemed to Griff. Her family. Her hometown. The great State of Texas. The young, the elderly, the less fortunate. Griff had learned very early on that Julia Sennett was an individual of incomparable conviction and standards. And he came to love her for those qualities and all that she was besides.

That was why he'd carefully hidden that love. Griff had known early on that Reb cared for Julia, too, in as special a way. The undercurrent, at least to Griff's perception, had always been there, along with the possibility that their friendship would be affected. Because it had become slowly apparent to him— and to Reb, too, he was sure—that the bond between Julia and himself was something a little more special, a little deeper, than her bond with Reb. Things had come to a point, though, where some rift was inevitable, because Griff wanted Julia.

He swallowed, hard, mentally cursing the masochist in him that had led him to this ground tonight. For even now, he ached for her. She was the only girl he'd ever wanted, the only girl he'd ever loved.

And while friendship was friendship, at fifteen he hadn't been about to let his chance with her pass by.

But he'd waited just a little too long to declare himself.

He remembered the day clearly. The three of them had been goofing around one of the county fairground corrals after the junior rodeo, the two boys doing their standard parsing of every other rider's performance, since Griff or Reb usually traded off taking the top two slots in bronc riding.

Reb, Griff recalled, hadn't had a good day, hadn't been able to catch a break worth a lick, while he'd had one of the best rides of his life. The cherry on the top had been getting down off of that wild pony and glancing over to the stands to where Julia had been hooting and hollering her head off....

LEANING HIS FOREARMS on the top rail, he stood next to Julia and allowed his gaze to be frankly admiring.

She was sitting on the fence rail, beside him, looking good enough to eat in a new pair of Wrangler jeans and a straw Stetson that made her hazel eyes glow beneath the brim.

"That was one heckuva ride you had today,

cowboy," she said at the break in the conversation.

"I always seem to do better when you're watching," he replied significantly.

She reached down to flick some nonexistent dust from his shirtsleeve in a way that could only be labeled as flirtatious, making his heart beat like a brass band.

He glanced past her only to find Reb observing them both. Griff held his friend's gaze steadily, the message clear.

There was a challenge in Reb's eyes. He'd never seen it before and would probably remember it for the rest of his life.

"Hey, they put one of the bulls in the next enclosure," Reb said abruptly. "I bet I could get aboard him and hang on long enough to make an eight count."

"Usin' what to hang on?" Griff drawled, not taking his friend seriously. Not at all wanting to leave Julia's side.

Reb held up a long, wide leather strap with a buckle on it. "I borrowed this bull-riding gear from one of the waddies."

"You mean you stole it!" Julia said, scandalized.

Reb scowled. "I'll give it back. I just want to try some of the moves I've been practicin' on a real bull. Broncs ain't for me, anyway. Too easy."

Lately Reb had been taking a stab at learning to ride bulls, obviously a result of falling behind his friend at bronc riding. Griff didn't think Reb was anywhere near ready to try his luck on a living, snorting animal.

"This isn't the time to go live, Reb," he said. "Why not wait till you've had a few more lessons 'fore you climb aboard a bull that's not electric. That way your daddy and I can be there to spot you and make sure you're set up right."

It had been the wrong thing to do, portray himself as the wiser, more experienced of the two.

"I can set myself up just fine, just watch!" Reb asserted, taking off across the corral to the enclosure where the Angus bull, Griff had to admit, stood grazing pretty darn peacefully. However, every Texan, male and female, had learned on their daddy's knee never to underestimate what stock, be it equine or bovine, might do in any given situation.

"No, Reb. It's too dangerous," Julia called after him. "Don't take chances like that, please."

"Takin' chances is what's gonna make

me a world champion bull rider someday."
He flung the words over his shoulder as he
marched hell-bent toward the bull.

Clearly, Reb was not thinking, was intent
on showing himself better than Griff—intent
on impressing Julia at any cost.

"Griff, stop him," she said, apparently not
realizing that this showdown was all for her.
She turned pleading hazel eyes on him. He
couldn't say no if he'd wanted to.

He started after his friend. "Reb, come on.
You're not gonna be able to even get near that
bull to put gear on him."

Reb pretended not to hear him as he
reached the fence and was over it in one leap.

Griff got really tense. Durn it, he knew he
shouldn't have been so blatant with the way
Julia was taken with him! This was Reb, his
best friend in the whole world. He didn't want
to be the kind of guy who one-upped his best
friend about anything.

"Reb, come back here!" he yelled, hus-
tling over the fence after him. The bull was
definitely taking an interest now in the half-
grown cowboy coming toward him across the
paddock. "Reb!"

"Listen to Griff, Reb! You're gonna get
yourself killed!"

Griff ventured a glance behind him at Julia, who'd rushed across the corral and was now clinging to the rail of the paddock fence, watching the two boys fearfully....

WHAT HAD HAPPENED next had always been a blur to Griff. He remembered calling after Reb again. This apparently had stirred up the bull, enough so that the beast had lowered his massive head threateningly and given a warning snort. And still Reb had approached the animal, albeit with some caution, his arms extended as if he'd somehow thought he had a chance at cornering the Angus. But then— and this was the hazy part for Griff—the bull had charged his friend. Griff could recall screaming Reb's name, could vaguely recollect making a mad dash to tackle him to roll them both out of the bull's path.

But at the last second sanity must have kicked in and Reb dived out of the way— leaving Griff to take a knife-sharp horn, backed by a thousand pounds of muscle, clear through his right thigh.

He'd been lucky, he later learned from the doctors, that he hadn't been gored in the abdomen, or the wound would have been fatal, for sure.

Griff lifted his beer to his lips but didn't drink. His convalescence had been long and hard. Reb and Julia had come to visit him in the hospital—Reb, in fact, had barely left his bedside the first four days, although Griff had been so high on painkillers he hardly even known his parents were there, let alone Reb.

Once the haze had cleared some, though, there'd been no avoiding the fact that his right leg had been damaged beyond complete repair. That he would always walk with a limp. That he would never compete in the rodeo again.

At fifteen, it had been a hard blow to take, to be sure. But it had been nothing compared to what had come next, and that something he would never forget. For when Griff had finally walked into high school on crutches four months later, he could see plain as day the real loss he'd bear for the rest of his life: his two best friends were holding hands.

Reb Farley had won Julia Sennett.

Griff coughed, rousing himself out of his reverie and taking a long, hard, deep draft of beer. He found it not without its own irony that his right leg had grown stiff as he'd stood there in the cold. He rubbed the heel of his hand down the length of his thigh muscle to loosen it up, and was glad for the deep ache his action produced.

Better there than a couple of feet north, in the vicinity of his heart, he figured, turning to head back into the house—and toward the part of his heart where the terrain didn't hold as many dangerous byways.

WHEN JULIA ARRIVED, the meeting room at the church hall was already filled with people talking excitedly about Reb Farley and what it meant to the entire town of Bridgewater to be able to recognize one of its sons as a rodeo world champion.

And from the sounds of it the bottom line was, they must make this one hell of a celebration.

She stepped to one side of the entryway, into the shadows, to try to collect herself. Up until today, she hadn't minded the hashing and rehashing of Reb's ride, which everyone had watched on a TV that had been set up in this very hall. Reb's parents, Sue and Gary, had actually flown to Las Vegas to be there for their son. Julia had stayed behind, as always. She couldn't watch Reb compete. She'd gone to one rodeo in his first season on the pro circuit. He'd done well—but watching him had brought back in living color that moment when she'd seen both Reb and Griff go flying through the air in two different directions, only to come crashing down in a dusty welter of legs, hats and hooves.

And ending with Griff lying in the dirt as if dead, blood darkening his torn jeans around the gash in his thigh.

"You'd think the Reverend Billy Graham was comin' to town," an amused voice said into her ear. "Or his boss."

She glanced around to find Griff wearing a bemused smile as he perused the gathering.

She was so glad he was here! She didn't think she'd make it through the meeting without him.

"Would you look at the crowd?" she said. "I'm beginning to wonder if there's anyone in town who *won't* be involved in pulling this celebration together."

"Reb Farley winning the gold buckle in bull riding is the biggest thing that's happened to Bridgewater," Griff said. "Everyone wants to be able to tell their kids and grandkids they played a hand in welcoming him home in style."

They shared a glance that spoke volumes to Julia.

"Which is to say there's no way to get out of this," she said with a sigh.

He gave her elbow a squeeze. "Just remember, I'm here to help however I can."

"Then consider this a major S.O.S." she muttered out of the corner of her mouth as Alma Butters, Bridgewater's self-proclaimed doyenne, caught sight of the two of them standing at the doorway.

"Here's Reb's bride-to-be and his best man now!" she exclaimed, steaming toward to them with the purposefulness of the *QE II*— and guaranteeing her unimpeded passage.

At Alma's pronouncement, Julia stifled a groan. Alma Butters was the busiest body in town. How was she going to keep up a facade that all was well with herself and Reb when it wasn't? She'd give Alma five minutes to sniff out the fact that something wasn't right with the engaged couple.

This plan of Griff's was insane! She'd never been good at dissembling, never had even a white lie cross her lips without the guilt written all over her face giving her away.

She felt that warm, reassuring pressure on her arm again.

"Don't worry, Julia," Griff murmured. "We'll handle Alma and the rest just fine."

His confidence did help. Maybe she could absorb it through her arm like osmosis.

"Evening, ma'am," Griff said, exaggerating his drawl as the other woman docked squarely in front of Julia. "What a nice turnout we've got here tonight, no doubt due to your efforts."

Julia watched as he loaded up his smile with pure cowboy charisma and launched it at the older woman, who looked as stunned as if she'd really taken a hit right between the eyes.

"I made some phone calls, it's true," Alma demurred.

"Well, we're much obliged." Griff cocked his head. "Wait a sec… Are you doin' something different with your hair to make your face look so rosy and your eyes so bright?"

She blushed another three shades of red under the full bore of his charm as Julia choked back a giggle. Alma's steel-gray beehive hairdo was famous for being indestructible, even in a Texas headwind. Changing it would have required a hammer and chisel.

"My word, no," Alma answered. "I must be flushed from taking a coffee cake from the oven in the church kitchen."

"That's what smells so good!" Griff declared. Giving Julia a covert wink, he took

Alma's arm. "I'd surely appreciate it if you'd cut me a piece of that cake yourself."

"Well, all right, Griff." Alma actually fanned herself as she allowed him to escort her over to a table a few feet away that groaned with the food and coffee requisite at any Texas gathering of two or more people.

Looking after them, Julia shook her head. She'd not met the female yet who could resist Griff's rakish grin and violet-blue eyes when he chose to put them to use.

Bless him for taking Alma on. Yet the score was but one down, with scads more to go as Julia was blindsided by a bear hug.

"Here's our girl!" enthused Gary Farley, Reb's father. His mother, Sue, was close behind with a squeeze of her own for their future daughter-in-law.

Julia hugged Sue back as tears stung her eyes. Did Sue and Gary Farley know of their son's intentions regarding her? she wondered wildly. She loved Reb's parents dearly and would have hated to disappoint them, would hate to be the cause of their disappointment in their son.

But they seemed blessedly in the dark on that score as Gary gazed at her fondly. "When are you comin' over for supper so you can see the video I shot of Reb's ride? I know you don't like to watch him compete, but this is one time when you know the ending's gonna turn out all right. Of course, the tape don't show the half of what went on. I was jumpin' up and down and hollerin' the whole time."

"Soon." Julia gave them a one-word promise, which was about all she felt confident enough to muster. Anything more and she feared they'd spot something of the deception she and Griff were trying to pull off.

It seemed Reb's mother had detected the slight hesitation in her answer, even if Sue was off track on its cause.

"I know you have a hard time watchin' Reb ride," she told Julia with a pat on her arm. "We all're scared for him sometimes. But that's the life of a rodeo cowboy. I imagine you'll get used to him havin' such a dangerous job once you're married. You're bound to watch him ride more, and it might help calm your fears to see him take a bad tumble or two and come out all right."

Would it, though? Julia wondered. She didn't think she'd ever get "used" to even thinking about Reb climbing atop the back of a two-thousand-pound, snorting-mad bull. Although he had never made an issue of her coming to watch him ride, she had always known deep down that her absence disappointed him.

But he knew why she couldn't be there— she had already witnessed one of her best friends nearly get killed by a bull. She did not want to see Reb go down, and there was always that risk. It was, literally, the nature of the beast.

She came out of her brief preoccupation to find Griff's gaze on her as he stood with Alma a few yards away. He'd obviously heard Sue's comment, and she realized that she hadn't echoed Reb's mother's sentiments.

And the way he looked at her…it made her feel as if he knew her thoughts intimately.

She glanced away, belatedly answering Sue with a noncommittal murmur as, strangely, guilt assailed her again, although this was of a different nature than the kind she experienced being evasive with Reb's parents.

"That reminds me, Griff," Alma's voice carried to her. "My grandniece is coming to stay with me for a month or so to see how she likes this part of Texas."

Julia's ears perked up even as she continued her conversation with Reb's parents. Out of the corner of Julia's eye she could see Alma had discerned that she had a captive audience in Griff Corbin, and she wasn't about to waste it. She rarely got into a dialogue in which she wasn't either mining for information or calling her own matters of interest to attention—and ambushing the listener into doing whatever she wanted.

It looked as if the latter was on her mind as she continued. "She graduated from college earlier this month and is plain up in the air about where she'd like to settle. Michele— that's her name, and a right pretty one, don't you think?—she's a nurse, and since your cousin Lara seems to be bringin' in more and more patients to the clinic, maybe another nurse would be affordable. I can tell you from experience they need another one down there, and Michele would be perfect for the job... that is, if we all can persuade her to come live in this backwater we call Bridgewater."

She actually tittered at her small joke.

Julia strained to hear Griff's murmured response but couldn't quite catch it.

"What?" she said abruptly to Reb's mother, who'd just asked her a question.

"I only was wondering if you and your brother and daddy would like to spend Christmas Day at our house, even though Reb won't be home till later in that week," Sue repeated.

"I'm sorry." Julia gave her a smile of apology, half an ear still on the other conversation. "Of course, I'd love to. I'm sure Daddy and Ty would, too."

"We thought we'd invite Griff and Frannie, too. It's been a while since all three families have done something together—"

"—especially since Michele is just your type—" Alma was prattling on. "Petite and dark-eyed, and game for just about anything."

Oh, no. So that was what Alma was up to: Griff's diverting her on Julia's behalf had put him neatly into the older woman's clutches. Historically, Julia knew, he liked to do his own asking when it came to getting dates, although such events were few and far between. She'd simply never seen a woman who'd piqued Griff's interest enough for him to pursue her for long.

Well, she'd have to see if she could break away from Reb's parents to rescue him.

Except, it occurred to Julia with a jolt, Griff didn't look as though he wanted rescuing as he answered rather loudly, as if making a point, "I've always thought I didn't really have a 'type,' but I've always liked women with a lot of pluck."

Griff's enthusiastic response apparently surprised Alma, for she was a few seconds long on the uptake.

"That's Michele to a T! And just as sweet as can be—"

"That sounds wonderful, Sue. Oh!" Julia made a show of looking at her watch. "Is it that time already? We should get started."

She excused herself and came up to stand next to Griff just as Alma was going in for the coup de grâce.

"Say, Griff, Michele will be here for Reb's party on New Year's Eve. I'd be real obliged if you'd escort her to the festivities."

"Well now, Alma, maybe a spirited gal like your grandniece might not want to step out with one of this backwater's native sons?" he drawled with apparent self-deprecation, so that Julia had no appreciation of how he really felt about Alma's attempt at matchmaking.

"Oh, you're just bein' modest," Alma said in response to his comment. "Any girl would be thrilled to be seen on your arm! I mean, maybe you're not a rodeo champion like Julia's Reb, but there's still a passel of girls in town who'd come a-runnin' at the crook of your finger. I daresay that hobble in your get-along is part of the attraction."

Chapter Three

Julia stifled a gasp of shock as she watched Griff's expression close up tight. How dare Alma embarrass him that way! Griff's slight limp was so much a part of him, no one even noticed it anymore, let alone talked about it.

"Oh, I don't think Griff's attraction's got anything to do with rodeoing *or* any kind of hobble." She leapt to his defense.

Alma at least had the grace to blush in shame. "I didn't mean it that way," she avowed.

Julia shot Griff a glance and found he was gazing at her with that same expression of earlier in the day—that smoldering intensity that fairly shouted a warning—making her defend him to Alma even more.

"It's that whole unattainable, inscrutable manner he's got going. *That's* what drives the women crazy."

She immediately regretted her attempt at humor when he said, "Do tell. So you think I ought to take Alma up on her offer?"

The full bent of his attention was on her, as if her opinion were of utmost importance to him, and she was dismayed to find herself in the position of having to feign enthusiasm for the notion. "What could it hurt?"

"Truly, I meant nothin' ill toward you, Griff," Alma broke in, "but it's not like you've got any other gal on the string right now."

"Too true," Griff allowed without apparent rancor.

Smelling a victory that had nearly been snuffed out cold, Alma pressed on. "Wouldn't it be nice to walk into your best friend's homecoming celebration with a pretty girl? So much better than goin' it alone."

His gaze still on Julia, he didn't answer Alma, only waited, as if he had all the time in the world, although she could tell Alma had picked up on the undercurrent between them.

Julia was at a loss. It was as if he wanted some reaction from her that she simply wasn't providing. Did he want her to disagree with Alma? Defend him and whatever choice he might make?

But he had made no choice, and it was purely frustrating, as it always was with him.

Finally she said, "It might be good for you to spend less time with your cows for a little female companionship."

There was an interminable beat of time, then he nodded, finally abandoning his scrutiny of her as he turned to Alma. "You're right, Alma. It would be nice. It'd be my pleasure to take Michele to Reb's celebration. I'm all for havin' fun."

"Won't that be dandy!" Alma effused with a of her hands. "Now, what say we get down to business?"

But as everyone took their seats, Julia had the strangest impression that the real business Alma had come here to transact had already taken place, quite to her satisfaction.

And it was obviously to Griff's satisfaction, as well.

JULIA WELCOMED THE snap of cold air that hit her in the face as she exited the church hall at ten-thirty that evening. She had the wildest urge to scream just for the sheer release.

"That," Griff said from behind her, "was brutal."

She had to laugh as they climbed into his

pickup for the ride home. After much haranguing and hair-tearing, the committee had finally reached a consensus. The theme—heavily lobbied for by herself and Griff—was to be the impressively restrained "Congratulations to Bridgewater's Son." The celebration itself would be a potluck for which Alma would distribute assignments—"To keep certain people from bringin' the same old, tired casserole again"—and the beer, decorations and entertainment would come out of the town's coffers with a budget of five hundred dollars.

Of course, there were infinite details to be worked out, but Griff had effectively divvied them up among subcommittees.

Julia glanced over at him as he pulled out of the church parking lot.

"Sorry you volunteered your services?" she asked.

"Not a'tall." He shrugged within his sheepskin jacket. "Sorry you decided to go along with this plan to act as if everything was normal?"

Shoving her hands deep into the pockets of her fleece jacket, Julia lifted her shoulders, as well. "No." She hesitated. "After tonight, I realized I don't want to be the reason Reb's stock with the town takes a dive, which is what would happen if I told anyone he's having second thoughts. After all, it's not just the two of us involved here—there's Reb's family and mine, you and yours, the whole town. It's got me wondering what I'll say to people if it turns out even after talking that he really doesn't want to get married."

"Well, if there's one piece of advice I can give you, it's don't worry about what the whole town thinks," Griff said reasonably. "However you and Reb resolve your situation is no one's business but your own."

"That's just it, Griff." She huffed her frustration. "I don't know how it's going to end up between us right now."

She pondered her now-clasped hands, resting in her lap. "I guess that's what has me most worried. I don't want to lose Reb as a friend, and I'm greatly afraid that'll happen."

"You could never lose Reb as a friend, Julia," Griff told her. "Any more than you could lose me as a friend."

She bit her lip. She'd had time to think since Griff and she had come up with their plan, and it seemed she was having more and more doubts like the one she'd experienced at Sue Farley's comment.

Determined to be honest, she made herself confess, "Sure, but what could he be having doubts about that he'd believe there's even a possibility that we're not meant to marry? If it *is* meant to be, there should be nothing so great it could keep us apart."

She turned her head to stare out the window. "I'm just not sure I want to be with a man who might not feel I'm worth whatever it takes for us to be together."

The silence in the cab of the truck went on for some minutes, and Julia wondered if she'd been *too* honest. But this was Griff! If she couldn't be honest with him, her best friend, who could she be honest with, share her heart with?

Yet it seemed as if there'd been a shift in their friendship in the short time since this afternoon's talk. Something had changed. Actually she'd felt it as she'd stood in Kearney's Tack and Feed this afternoon, and again earlier this evening as she'd talked with Reb's mother. Griff had seemed to be waiting for some reaction from her, or some realization.

"Julia," he said quietly.

She turned back to him almost desperately. "Yes?"

"I'm not too keen on givin' advice, solicited or otherwise. Makes me uncomfortable as hell. But let me give you another bit of it." He frowned thoughtfully as he gazed straight ahead. "If you do what's right for you, Julia, then it won't matter what everyone thinks about the outcome. Including Reb," he added softly but significantly.

He slowed as he came to an intersection, even though there wasn't a car in sight. Little towns like Bridgewater rolled down the shades and shut up tighter than a tick after about 9:00 p.m. Everyone was at home, within which they lived the most important part of their lives.

Griff was right. Whatever happened between her and Reb would indeed cause a stir, but in the end everyone would go back to their lives. She would go back to her life.

She peered at her friend in the dim glow of the dashboard lights, which outlined his strong jaw and cheekbones, features she knew as well as her own. Yet after decades of friendship she still found Griff an enigma of sorts. On the one hand, she knew him so well that she could predict with precise accuracy what his reaction would be down to the eyelash in nearly any situation.

And yet there was far more about him she

didn't know. He wasn't one to talk much about himself or his feelings. Of course, not much bothered him. He was the most even-tempered, steady person she'd ever known. She'd learned to see that quality for both its good and bad sides. It was of eternal comfort to her to know that Griff was always there, her rock—and it frustrated her that, like a rock, he seemed impervious to the vagaries of human emotion that subjected everyone else.

Take earlier this evening for example, when Alma had virtually thrown her niece at Griff—and he'd caught the volley without a bit of hesitation. Julia hated to admit it, but she'd been jealous, and she didn't like that she had been one bit. Didn't like herself for being so.

Why wouldn't she want to see Griff meet some wonderful woman and fall in love? Or even just enjoy some female companionship for a while? Heaven knew she wasn't going to be the best of companions for him in the coming weeks.

"Thanks, Griff," she said abruptly.

"For what?"

"For being you. I've thought it often enough today, but haven't told you that I couldn't do this without you. You're a dear, dear friend to both me and Reb, and I love you for it."

He stared straight ahead. "You've got to know I'd do anything for you, Julia," he said in a low voice. "Anything."

She was on the verge of returning the sentiment when, coming to a stop at the curb, he announced unnecessarily, "Well, here's your house."

There was another moment of awkwardness, and Julia wondered how such a state could exist between herself and this man who was so much a part of her life, her history. She had that crazy impression again that somehow the possibility existed that she might lose him, too, when all was said and done.

On impulse, she leaned across the seat to give Griff a fond peck on the cheek. But it was also the exact moment he turned his head toward her, apparently intent on saying something else, his mouth open to utter the words.

Their lips met.

So startled was she that when she didn't immediately pull back, Julia had the singular experience of the warm, moist touch of Griff's mouth on hers. A jolt of electricity shot through her, its voltage spiking when he moved his head ever so slightly in a brushing motion that instantly sensitized every nerve in her body—and had her automatically yearning for more.

Almost against her will, she leaned in infinitesimally, somehow needing to maintain the contact. It was as if the very thing she'd feared a moment ago could be banished forever as long as this touch was sustained.

As if the enigmatic Griff Corbin had revealed himself to her at last.

"Griff?" The word came out in a sigh.

"Julia." The word came out in a growl. In a warning, causing sanity to hit her.

On a gasp of horror, Julia hauled herself backward so that she came up against the car door with a thud, her fingers pressed against her traitorous lips.

What was she *doing?* This was Griff, for heaven's sake. Her best friend!

"Griff, I'm sorry," she choked. What would he think of her?

He hadn't moved an inch. "There's no need to apologize," he said. In the dim light his violet-blue eyes were like two gemstones glowing from within. Their expression made her want to run for the hills. Made her want to slide back across the seat to experience that wild connection again.

She was glad for the darkness as her cheeks flamed with embarrassment. Julia gave a nervous laugh. "That kiss was obviously an accident. Obviously."

No, she must be honest with him. "Either that or I'm more shaken up by Reb's letter than I thought."

"You have a right to be shaken up, Julia," he said in that same low voice, although she had the strangest impression he meant by their kiss and not by Reb's doubts.

And if so, she needed to take a page from Griff's book and get a firm grip on herself. Because she couldn't use his friendship and comfort to satisfy her need to feel wanted and desirable.

Most of all, though, she couldn't use Griff that way. Couldn't hurt him that way.

The mere thought brought tears to her eyes.

He saw them, of course, and immediately his features softened. "Julia, come on," he said with a teasing wheedle in his voice she'd heard a million times. She wasn't sure she could take it right now. "It wasn't *that* bad, was it? I mean, not like that time when we were seven and eye-level to Old Man Howe's hound dog, who'd taken such a shine to you he followed you all over town just to find the chance to catch you unawares and give you a big, wet sloppy kiss right across the mouth."

"That dog was a public nuisance," Julia said emphatically, remembering.

"But he didn't bother anyone else—just you," Griff reminded her. He tilted his head to one side. "Say, didn't he used to sit outside your house and bay at your window, too? I can promise you now I won't do anything like that."

She rolled her eyes at him tolerantly but couldn't help giggling. It was just like Griff to get her laughing in spite of herself, diffusing the awkward moment.

Yet completely forgetting his kiss wouldn't happen so easily. She was still experiencing its lingering effects, making her stomach flutter…making her heart flutter.

"Well, I'd better be getting inside," she murmured, giving herself one more reason to feel ashamed as she yanked open the door and piled out of his pickup with a hastily delivered goodbye.

But she simply couldn't stay in that truck with Griff.

Stumbling through her front door, she closed it and pressed her back up against it as she tried to catch her breath, tried to calm her heartbeat.

Tried not to cry again for the sheer confusion of it all.

JULIA HAD NEVER been so happy to hear a bell ring in all her life.

"That's it for today, class. Remember, you've got five arithmetic problems and ten vocabulary words to learn for tomorrow. I'll be here for another hour if anyone wants to stay for help with those."

As luck would have it, she delivered her words to the backs of eighteen second-graders who were as cheered as she was with the end of the school day. Normally she loved her job. Right now, however, Christmas break, which started next week, couldn't come a moment too soon.

With a sigh, she shoved the stack of social studies quizzes she had to correct this evening into her briefcase and was just about to lock up when a small head capped by short auburn hair peeked around the doorjamb.

"I could use a little help with my arithmetic, Miss Sennett," said the eight-year-old girl. "If you've got time, I mean."

Julia hid a smile. It was a familiar routine,

one she had grown fond of, truthfully. "Of course I've got time, Kelly. Come right in."

The girl virtually skipped to the front of the room to take a seat beside her.

A teacher wasn't to have favorites, and so Julia hid it well just how much this particular child meant to her. Perhaps it was how much the girl reminded her of herself at that age—independent to a fault, indignant of any false word or deed by others. Or by herself.

"So, which of these problems is givin' you fits?" Julia asked, opening the workbook on her desk.

Kelly chewed on the end of her pencil, pondering the decision. "Mmm…I guess the subtraction."

"Subtraction it is, then," Julia said, turning to that page.

Yet the little girl stalled, gazing up at her with startlingly green eyes. "Why's subtraction so hard, do you think? Addition's lots more…friendly. The numbers are all wantin' to get along with each other. With subtraction, it's always 'take away this much' or 'less that much.'"

Kelly frowned in thought. "It makes me sad. It's like you're havin' to give up what you thought was yours to keep."

Julia couldn't help it. She laughed. "I'm sorry, Kelly," she immediately apologized. "I guess I never thought of it like that, but yes, subtraction is a little sad—as if you're breaking up a family."

She bent to touch her forehead to the girl's. "Just wait till division, when numbers don't just get taken away, they get broken into little pieces. That'll *really* send you for a loop."

To her dismay, Kelly didn't smile at her joke. Instead she looked as if she were about to cry.

"I'm sorry, Kelly. I was only kidding." She put her arm around the child's shoulders.

"It's not anything you said," Kelly confessed. "Honest." She ducked her head briefly, and when she tipped her face back up to Julia's there were tears in her big green eyes.

"What is it, dear?" Julia asked in concern.

"I didn't wanna see you 'cause of my arithmetic. It's…it's Jace Gentry— I mean Larrabie. I like him—but I don't think he likes me, not that way."

Aha. Boy trouble. Of course, what else would it be?

"He's pretty cute, isn't he?" Julia said solemnly.

"And really nice," the girl agreed. "It's

kinda funny. I didn't know him very well in kindergarten or first grade. He kept to himself a lot. But now that his daddy's come back and married his mama, he's been talking more to people. Talking to me."

"Well, I'd think that's a good sign, don't you? That you can talk to each other. Many a romance starts out being friends."

She almost added, "Look what happened with Reb and me," but the words stayed on her tongue. Who knew what would happen with the two of them?

"Sure, but wouldn't I know if there was… somethin' there behind the friendship?" Kelly asked, her forehead creased in concentration. "Special feelings?"

"You might," Julia allowed, "but then again, you might not. Not right away. Some people just take longer to warm up to others. And after what Jace has been through, don't you think he has a right to hold his deeper feelings close until he knows you better?"

"I guess." She sighed. "So what do I do?"

"Just be yourself, Kelly," Julia told her, squeezing her shoulders. "And be patient. That's all you can do."

It was good advice, the kind Griff had given her, but it clearly wasn't what Kelly wanted to hear. That was youth, however. You wanted to get from A to B—in this case from like to love—as quickly as possible. Julia guessed that Kelly would learn the hard way, at least the first time around. She could only hope that the little girl would take the lesson to heart, and the next time around appreciate how wonderful it could be to take one's time getting to be friends with a boy first, learning to love each other without the complication of romance, before introducing that element into the relationship.

And when one did, then it wasn't a complication at all. It was like icing on the cake, when the cake had been baked with care.

There was a knock at the classroom door, bringing Julia out of her thoughts.

She looked up as Griff glanced in.

"Hey, Teach. Got a minute for me?"

She was uncommonly glad to see him, despite that tense moment in his pickup a few nights ago. It really had been ridiculous. This was *Griff,* for heaven's sake! Her best friend in the world.

Still, she couldn't stop the flutter that again came to her stomach at the memory of his mouth against hers.

"Of course," she said. "Kelly and I are through here, aren't we?"

Kelly nodded, clearly still downcast but with some good food for thought to chew on in the next few days. She stuck her workbook into her backpack and waved a goodbye to her teacher and to Griff as she passed him on her way out the door.

Julia gazed after her, shaking her head, before turning to Griff. He had on his work clothes of faded Wrangler jeans, dusty cowboy boots and sheepskin vest over a flannel shirt in a look that was undiluted cowboy. She'd seen him dressed so thousands of times, but for some reason the picture he made, with that perennial five o'clock shadow and his Stetson shading his violet-blue eyes in such a way it made them prismatic, made another of those thrills flit through her stomach.

"What brings you into town at this hour?" she asked, taking a calming breath and firmly putting the image out of her mind.

"The quotes came in for the sign that's to go up along the highway as you're comin' into town." At her blank look, he elaborated. "You know, the one about Bridgewater being home to Reb Farley, National Finals Rodeo Bull Riding Champion?"

"Oh! Yes, that sign." She'd completely forgotten that he'd said he would check on the matter this afternoon. "I guess I was concentrating so hard on Kelly's problem, it slipped my mind."

"Some kind of trouble?" Griff asked with a lift of his eyebrows.

"The worst kind—boys. I'm not one to tell tales out of school—or in it, as the case may be." She sighed as she stacked her teacher's guides. "Kelly's sweet on Jace Larrabie, but it seems he's either oblivious to her special feelings for him, or he knows and he's only interested in being friends with her."

Chin down, Griff seemed suddenly preoccupied with moving the glass apple-shaped paperweight on her desk a precise inch to the left. "So what advice did you give her?"

She lifted her shoulders. "What could I say? I wanted to be honest while still being hopeful, so I said that if anything's going to happen, she'll need to be patient, which is hard to do when you're eight."

He peered at her curiously from under the brim of his Stetson. "It's hard at any age."

"I guess she'll survive, just like everyone else in the world has," Julia admitted, wondering at his mood today. Very…cryptic.

"I just hope she won't get her heart broken should Jace not return her feelings."

Julia bit her lip, worrying. Kelly was a well-adjusted child, but as Griff said, love at any age was difficult.

I should know, she thought, experiencing a different sort of pang to her stomach.

"It's good, at least, that she has someone like you to be her sounding board," Griff put in when she was silent for several seconds.

She decided she wouldn't get a better opening. "Speaking of which…" She looked up at him. "I heard from Reb last night."

That now-familiar flare shot into his eyes at the mention of Reb. "You did?"

"He called from L.A., of all places. He's being wined and dined within an inch of his life by potential sponsors."

It had been such a strange conversation, she had a hard time recalling how it had gone. "It appears he's thinking of goin' with one of the smaller outfits, since he feels like he'd just be one in a stable of hundreds with some of those multinational companies."

Her gaze faltered. Given the advice he given her about doing what was right for her, she simply couldn't look Griff in the eye as she revealed, "I asked him about his letter, and he asked me to be patient. That he hadn't felt it right not to say anything until he got home, but that it was something that needed discussing in person. That's all he would say on the subject. Oh—he asked about you."

"Me?"

"Yes—what your reaction was." That part had been stranger still. "I told him of the plan we'd come up with…to wait till he got here before saying anything to families or friends."

"And?" He stepped closer, and she made herself look at him.

"Actually, he thought that was a good idea. Which makes me think you may be right, and he's just trying to sort out what comes next in his life now that he's gotten what he's always wanted."

The thought made her feel…hollow inside. Yes, that was the emotion she'd been experiencing since Reb's call. So why did the thought that this bump in their relationship might be just that and nothing more make her feel hollow and blue? It should be good news. For some reason it wasn't, though.

"Oh, Griff!" she blurted all of a sudden, dropping into her chair and pushing her books aside. "Why is it I feel that something hasn't been right between Reb and me for a long time?" She pressed her palms to her cheeks in her confusion, which it seemed she was feeling a lot lately—more than she'd ever felt in her life. And it wasn't a feeling she relished.

Griff slid one hip next to her onto the desk. "What do you mean?" he asked softly. How glad she was he was here right now!

"The other evening," she explained, "when Reb's mother said something about my getting used to the dangers of Reb's profession, I realized that no, I would never get used to him risking his life for a living!"

She blinked her disbelief. "I honestly can't fathom how it is that I didn't contemplate that fact even once! And it's got me wondering if *that* is what's given me this…inkling that something has always made me doubt just a little bit whether Reb and I would be truly happy together."

At her words, Griff stood. When she looked up at him in inquiry, she saw that he'd become uncommonly still, for some reason. Uncommonly stiff.

"I think it's a good idea to really think the matter over," he said. "Like I said, you deserve the best, Julia."

"And I'm still not certain that Reb can't provide me that." She stood, as well, mildly alarmed at his demeanor. He was so…tense, as if he were holding himself back from doing or saying something.

"I'm just so afraid I'm going to lose him as a friend, no matter what we decide," she said again on a rush of emotion, a rush of anxiety that she couldn't get to the root of. "I—I know you told me that couldn't happen, but I have this niggling feeling that something awful *is* bound to happen—and I don't mean in the rodeo ring."

She spread her hands. "I mean, how could Reb and I go back to being just friends after being engaged? I don't think it works that way. I don't think people's emotions work that way. And if we *can't* be friends after this… I don't think I could stand it, Griff."

In fact, the thought made that hollowness inside her spread like a virus, and she dropped her chin again, miserably close to tears, miserably confused.

She'd rarely felt so before: searching, mostly within herself, for direction. Not that she found such searching distressing; she'd learned it meant she was growing in some way. But it also meant that, deep within her, she was dissatisfied with the way some situation in her life was going—and that change, whether she wanted it to or not, was bound to occur.

Two boots appeared in her line of sight, and she lifted her head. Although she and Griff were closer than they'd been in his truck the other night, his expression was as unfathomable as ever.

And still he was tense, she could tell. As much as she didn't know about her friend, she knew this: he loved her and Reb like his own flesh and blood, and to see his friends unhappy was hard on him.

She wanted badly to reach out to him—in friendship, nothing more. She wanted him to reach out to her.

And it seemed he might, for a split second. Seemed he might say something that would make everything come clear to her.

"Look, Jules," he finally said. "Like I said, I'm all for you thinkin' things over good and hard, so that you know what it is you want to do…what it is you're wanting in your life."

"I was j-just thinking that exact thing," Julia said, her voice catching with relief. Oh, the situation *couldn't* be as desperate or confusing as she'd thought, not with Griff here to help her sort it out.

Except then he went on, as impassively as she'd ever known him to be, "Good, because I'm gonna have to bow out as *your* sounding board."

Chapter Four

Griff watched Julia's mouth fall open from out-and-out surprise, out-and-out disappointment. Out-and-out hurt. It made him immediately want to take back the words.

They were already spoken, however. That was the hazard in such things, and why he had remained silent for so long.

"But…you said we'd get through this together," she said, her voice soft in her bewilderment.

"And I'm still committed to bein' there for you. I'm just not gonna be there when you do your soul-searching about Reb. I can't be."

"But why, Griff?"

He glanced away, unable to meet her eyes and have her discover the truth in his. Yes, why? What reason on earth could he give her, his most cherished friend, for not standing by her every step of the way? Wasn't that what friends did for each other, even if it meant taking a few hits to the solar plexus himself?

The problem was, he might be Julia's friend, but he wanted to be the man she loved, and the two were mutually incompatible, at least in this situation where she was working through her feelings about his *other* best friend. He'd only realized how impossible it was the evening of their kiss, if one could even begin to call that briefest of contacts a kiss.

Oh, you sure could, cowboy, the voice in his head told him. He'd almost thought he'd gotten away with walking that particular razor's edge by accepting Alma Butters's invitation to ask her grandniece to the celebration. Maybe by focusing his and everyone else's attention away from the interaction between himself and Julia, he'd be able to keep his promise to her—and to himself.

But then there'd been his reaction to the feel of Julia's soft lips against his that had been every bit as exciting and soul-stirring as the deepest of kisses. It had been more than how the caress made him feel, though—it was Julia's reaction, as well. He *knew* she'd been as stirred as he. He'd seen it in the melting of her eyes, heard it in the sigh of his name.

Yet it wouldn't have been right to take unfair advantage of her that way, in a moment of her vulnerability and weakness. In a moment of his. Besides, he didn't want that sort of connection with her unless the true-blue, deep and abiding feelings of love were behind it.

Still, it had taken everything in him to ward her away from taking it one step further.

"Let's just say that while you're tryin' to do what's best for yourself, I'm tryin' to do what's best for you, too," he finally told her, making a conscious effort to keep his voice and features relaxed and reassuring, as the friends they were to each other.

It wasn't working, though. "And this would be best?" she asked, hazel eyes searching. "I—I need you, Griff. I know in most things I've just blazed ahead on my own, and the unwritten routine is that you'll follow along and help me with whatever cause I've taken into my head to pursue."

She spread her hands, palms down, on the desk. "But *this*…this is different." Her eyes closed briefly. "I'm not all that confident or sure of myself."

He knew how hard it was for her to admit such a thing, even to him. "You'll be fine, I know it," he said, meaning it. "Besides, I'm still committed to bein' there for you. Just… not when you're figurin' out how you feel about Reb." He paused. "Try and understand, Julia. Reb's my friend, too."

He could see she was not convinced, was still hurt and confused by what she must consider a breach of friendship. So how to make her understand there was a greater promise of friendship he must keep, for both their sakes?

He took a deep breath, thinking again that he should have kept his mouth shut, should keep it shut now, but she had to understand.

Unable to stop himself, he reached out and set his hand over hers as it rested on her desk. "*You're* my friend," he said quietly, "and I'd never let you do anything to betray him."

He hoped to heaven that he'd made his point, because he wasn't sure he could say much else without declaring himself.

He apparently succeeded, though, for her hazel eyes rounded not only in shock, but also in understanding.

The color rose to her cheeks, and he wondered at the emotion that was its source.

Embarrassment, certainly, but as a result of having acted foolishly or falsely?

"You're talking about that...that accidental kiss," she said with that frankness he prized in her—except at this moment.

He cleared his throat. "Yes."

"That was *entirely* my fault," she said fervently. "I take full responsibility for it. You didn't have anything to do with it. Honestly, don't make that the reason you don't feel comfortable with me! Believe me, Griff—it *won't* happen again. There's no chance of it."

That set him to pointing his gaze on anything else in the room but her.

So. On the one hand, it was clear Julia hadn't grasped the extent of his feelings for her, and he was glad to be spared that complication. But it was also pretty clear she had no clue he felt anything for her at all of the romantic nature—and had actually been made uncomfortable by the very prospect of it!

And for that, Griff didn't know whether to be glad or not, speculating just moments after he'd debated whether to speak at all if perhaps he *should* have brought things completely out in the open and dealt with the consequences.

Well, he still had that opportunity.

But before he could speak, Julia surprised

him by turning her palm upward to lace her fingers in his, and for a tense moment Griff wondered if he'd been mistaken. Perhaps *she* did know what he felt for her and would speak with that frankness that was so much a part of who she was.

She only nodded, however. "I'll do whatever you think best, Griff. If not confiding in you right now is what you want, then I'll do it. I couldn't stand it, *especially* right now, if I caused a rift in our friendship."

More than ever, he found her touch electrifying, while his, apparently, still seemed to her as comfortably friendly as ever. The realization solidified his determination.

Gently he extracted his hand from hers with a pat. "I don't think it's a matter of what I want," Griff said. "I'm just tryin' to take a page from my own book—and do what's best for me, too."

And on that, he turned and walked out of the classroom, walked away from Julia. Barring the months of physical therapy after his accident, it was the hardest thing he'd ever done.

Especially when he heard the uneven echo of his own boot heels on the polished linoleum floor as he headed down the deserted corridor. It was an exceedingly lonesome sound.

RUNNING LATE FOR her meeting, Julia reached the door of the church hall just as Griff's mother did.

"Well, hello, Julia!" Frannie Corbin greeted her with a warm hug. "Strange, I don't think I've seen you since Reb rode away with the world championship."

"That *is* strange, given Bridgewater's not got a whole lot of places to hide," Julia laughed, hugging her back. Griff's mother was one of the nicest people she knew, had practically been a second mother to her after Julia's own had died.

"Oh, I haven't been hiding, by any means," Frannie said, opening the front door and preceding Julia through it to the vestibule. "Have you?"

"Not...exactly," Julia murmured without explanation. It was just that, ever since she and Griff had had that talk in her classroom nearly a week ago, she *had* been avoiding the places in town he frequented and the times he might be there. She simply couldn't think of another way to keep her word to Griff, because she wanted to confide in him as she always had, now more than ever.

She wished they had never shared that accidental kiss! Sure, it had raised some feelings in her that were at worst awkward to manage. She had come to the firm conclusion that the thrill she had experienced was more a reaction to the uncertain situation between her and Reb than anything deeper or more complicated that might lead to betraying one's friend and fiancé. But how to prove that to Griff? She simply couldn't let the friend she needed to lean on most to get through the next few weeks continue to feel that she was someone he should stay away from.

Oh, she hated living like this! She'd already found it taxing to keep Reb's doubts a secret from their families, and now this…this moratorium on confiding to Griff about the very matters she most needed the help of his particularly attuned ear to work through. More than that, she just plain missed him. Hardly ever had he not been a part of her day-to-day life—just that year she'd been in Central America with the Peace Corps, and the months after that when he'd gone to work on a ranch up north. And she'd missed him then, too, terribly. Combined with everything else she was dealing with, his absence in her life had succeeded in making her as sensitive as a bad sunburn.

She slid out of her jacket and hung it next to

Frannie's as she continued to chat with Griff's mother with half her mind. Perhaps Frannie's presence here might mean that Griff had decided to sit out the last planning meeting, since of course her own attendance was required. She couldn't help but feel a little disappointed. She'd been half hoping tonight's meeting meant she would see him for sure.

But it appeared her hope had materialized—or at least partly so—for as she entered the hall she spied Griff on the other side, sitting negligently in one of the side chairs against the wall, one booted ankle resting on the knee of his other leg.

Her heart lifted with gladness at seeing him. Darn it, she didn't care if all the two of them talked about was the price of beef, she wasn't going to cut a swath around him to avoid the two of them encountering each other!

But just as Julia was about to excuse herself and go to him, a pretty, petite young woman who could only be Alma Butters's niece Michele walked over and fairly plunked herself down at his side.

She smiled up at him, her lips moving as she murmured something, and he actually smiled back as he said a few words in reply.

Whatever those words were, Julia would bet the ranch they weren't about the price of beef.

"Goodness, Julia, you look like you've just seen a ghost!" Griff's mother remarked.

With what seemed a Herculean effort, Julia tore her gaze away from the couple, only to stare blankly at Griff's mother.

"W-what have I seen?" she asked inanely.

"A ghost. Or something as unexpected." Frannie scrutinized her with such thoroughness Julia blushed.

"It's Griff," she blurted, simply unable to deceive his mother with some fabrication. "I didn't expect him to be here."

"So…it's a problem that he is?" Frannie asked in bewilderment.

"No!" Good grief, even when she tried to be honest she made a mess of things! "It's just…he's done so much already to help get this shindig together, I hope he doesn't feel he's got to do more."

Frannie peered at her intently. Her gaze shifted to her son, who at that moment, Julia noted, seemed as engrossed in the woman at his side as a boy with a new pony.

"I wouldn't worry about Griff. I think he's capable of decidin' what's best for him," Frannie said, making Julia whip around to stare at her in curiosity. Why would she use that particular phrase?

Yet Griff's mother only lifted her shoulders inculpably. "Come on." She took Julia's arm. "I can see Alma's chomping at the bit to get started. Talk about someone who could use takin' at least a few fingers out of all the pies she's got them in around town."

THE FIRST HOUR of the meeting passed in a relative blur for Julia. She registered that Schultzy Schultz reported that the food committee had arranged for Mac Fisher to provide all the barbecued beef, plus buns and fixings, for the party. That left the side dishes and desserts to be provided by volunteers, whom Alma had ably rounded up and directed to within an inch of their lives.

But everything became crystal clear for Julia shortly after Herm Batcher, chairman of the entertainment committee, started running through the three bands they were considering.

"They's all pret' near the same cost," he dutifully reported. "And us on the committee did just like y'all said and picked a variety of music these folks play. So's we got an oldies band to consider, a bunch of rock 'n' roll fellas, and of course your C and W band. It's just a matter of choosin' one to fit the mood."

That created a minor hubbub as everyone chimed in with their opinion about what kind of music the celebration for a rodeo champion called for, as if the president of the United States himself were the guest of honor.

"You know Reb best, Julia," Herm finally said with a film of desperation glazing his eyes. "What band do you think we oughta book?"

Inwardly, Julia groaned, wishing Reb's parents were here instead of at a holiday party for their bunko group. But then, even with them present, it always came down to her decision based upon her up-close-and-personal knowledge of Reb's likes and dislikes. It was a good thing this was the last meeting before the party on New Year's. She was definitely wearying of having to approve every little detail.

"Reb generally likes a band that people can dance to," she said, trying as she had all evening to keep her gaze from going to Griff. Michele had not left his side once.

"Well, we surely don't want a band no one can or cares to dance to," Alma pronounced, as if she were going to be doing most of the hoofing. "That'd put a damper on the celebration for everyone, not just Reb."

Her comment had Herm scratching his head. "I'm 'fraid I couldn't say whether any of the bands are danceable," he said defensively. "I know what *I* consider danceable, and it's probably not the same as you kids."

Apparently he spoke to Julia, Griff and Michele, who were the only people under thirty—if not forty—in the room, which evidently made them "kids."

Herm indicated a large envelope on the table in front of him. "I brought their demonstration tapes, though, if y'all want to take a listen."

This, Julia could tell Herm was relieved to see, was met with enthusiasm. Someone remembered that the Sunday school classes had a tape player they used to learn Bible songs, and went to fetch it. Herm popped in the first tape he laid his hands on, which happened to be the country band.

Within seconds, the upbeat tempo of the Tractors's "Boogie Woogie Choo-choo Train" had filled the room.

The lead singer on the tape did a good job with it, Julia thought, tapping her foot. But before he had gotten halfway through the first verse, Alma's grandniece asked over the music, "So, isn't anyone going to actually test out how good the band is to dance to?"

She glanced around, but obviously her question was meant to reach Griff's ears if no one else's.

It did. In fact, the tips of those ears turned red.

Julia stared at him. She'd never noticed that about him before. Or, now that she thought about it, she had, but hadn't registered it consciously. Half a dozen instances when she could recall a similar reaction in Griff sprang to her mind. Of course, like any cowboy who spent the majority of his waking hours on the range, he wore his hat nearly sunup to sundown. One didn't have ample opportunity to observe the varied shades and colors a cowboy's ears might take on.

Or what those shades might mean, which, in Griff's case, seemed to be a weather vane of those closely held emotions of his. His ears turned even redder when Michele took his wrist and gave it a tug. "How about it, Griff?" she coaxed. "Just one spin around the floor?"

"Sorry. I'm not much for dancin', I'm

afraid," he returned stoically, gently removing his hand from her grasp.

Another realization struck Julia—that she had never seen Griff dance, nor even take a stab at it. Just as abruptly she knew why.

Her heart went out to him in empathy, but before she could physically react, Michele set her hands on her hips, attractively affecting disappointment. "Not one for dancin'? Now, I can't believe that!"

She pivoted to address her great-aunt. "Aunt Alma, Griff here says he's not one for dancin'."

Alma looked distinctly nonplussed, likely recalling her own recent gaff on the same subject.

"I think you might want to take him at his word, sugar," she hinted as around her people shifted in their seats, for they'd marked the problem at hand, as well. Beside her, Julia felt rather than saw Frannie stiffen.

No one said anything, however, so Michele had no way of knowing what everyone else knew. Julia was wondering madly how to apprise her of the situation when the young woman said gaily, "Not dance? What bull! I think you're pulling my leg, Griff Corbin!"

JULIA HID A wince as Griff's mother sucked in a breath. Could Michele have used a worse choice of words? Even her aunt's expression turned pained.

Herm stopped the tape and the absence of sound in the room echoed like a sonic boom.

"Michele, honey," Alma began, apparently meaning to explain, but she was interrupted by Griff's deep drawl.

"Bull's what it is, all right, and some leg-pulling, too, but not the kind you're referrin' to," he said, amusement tingeing his words. "You couldn't know, of course, Michele, but when I was a kid I got into a scrape with the business end of an Angus bull. The limp he left me with doesn't exactly make me the best dancin' partner in the world."

Michele gasped softly, completely stricken. "Oh! I'm so sorry! I wouldn't have pressed it if I'd've known there weren't any songs you could dance to."

The silence only grew more awkward, the tips of Griff's ears more scarlet, until Julia couldn't stand it any longer. Couldn't stand to see Griff embarrassed so.

"I bet there are," she said so suddenly it startled half the group.

"You'll bet there are what?" Frannie asked.

"That there *are* some songs you'd be good dancin' to, Griff. Like some of the slow ones. There's not much to do with your feet except a box-step."

Griff looked at her with a strange expression on his face. "I might could do that," he allowed, and it registered in her mind that he sounded not at all enthused. But Julia was too glad to be able to do something—something for Griff—to let that stop her.

"Why sure, you could! What's to stop you?"

"Nothing, I guess." He hesitated, then said in a strained voice, "I never tried before, is all."

She jumped to her feet. "Then let's try together! I'd be happy to help you."

She turned to Herm. "What's the next song on the tape?"

He fast-forwarded to Tim McGraw's ballad, "My Best Friend." *Perfect,* Julia thought.

She walked across the wooden floor and offered her hand to Griff.

"Are you sure you want to get into this with me, Julia?" he murmured, the look in his eyes as inscrutable as ever.

It made that strange flutter return to her

stomach, but she tamped it down. "You're *my* best friend, Griff. Why wouldn't I?"

He let her pull him to his feet and out onto the floor. Once there, however, he effectively took charge with an arm around her waist, tucking her hand into his larger one—before he pulled her against him almost roughly.

She looked up at him, surprised. His expression was as dispassionate as ever. But his eyes…again they almost glittered with the intensity of some emotion. Almost…anger, although not at her. Not entirely, in any case.

"All right then, Julia," he muttered. "Let's dance."

She could barely gather her scattered thoughts much less concentrate on how she should be moving her feet, but Julia managed to stammer, "W-we don't have to do anything fancy, not at this tempo. Maybe if we just start out swaying to the beat, so you get a feel for it. Then just go ahead and do what feels natural, and I'll follow your lead."

Taking her cue perfectly, Griff began by shifting his weight on to the tempo alternating feet, taking her along with him.

She gave him an encouraging smile. "That's it. Now, whenever you want to start movin' your feet…"

"You mean, like this?" he asked, and with a tightening of his arm around her waist, he took a short step to the side and then forward on a turn, smoothly sweeping her along with him.

"Y-yes," she said, feeling suddenly giddy. "You really do have a fine sense of rhythm, Griff."

"Like ridin' a buckin' bronco," he told her. "Reb'll tell you that. It's all in the timing."

It certainly was, she thought distractedly as the singer on the tape went on about having the best of two worlds by being in love with his best friend. She became hyper-aware of how their bodies brushed against each other, of how his arm around her felt so strong and secure, of how her hand seemed to fit so naturally into his. Of how they moved as one, as if they'd been born to dance this dance together.

It wasn't that she hadn't expected him to pick up the steps so quickly when he'd never tried dancing before. But given that he hadn't on account of his accident, just as he never would go back to rodeoing...

No, he'd never tried this kind of thing before, and it hit Julia like a load of bricks dropped from above that in all the time she'd known Griff, she'd never heard him speak of his accident or its effect on his life. And so she had forgotten that, along with Reb, he'd been an up-and-coming rodeo rider, had even taken a slight lead over Reb in ability. In fact, up until Griff's accident, the two friends practically ate, drank and slept rodeoing. Their hopes and dreams had been as one, it had seemed to her.

After the accident, though, she'd never heard Griff talk about the rodeo, not in terms of his own dreams, and she realized now how hard it must have been for him to give Reb the support he had. How much that experience at the age of fifteen had changed him from the boy who, while still one to always hold his emotions close to the vest, had been so much more warm and open.

Of course, the change wouldn't have been noticed by anyone who didn't know Griff well. As for Julia, if she hadn't recognized the difference in him, it was because in her eyes the accident hadn't changed him, either physically or emotionally. He was and always would be simply Griff to her.

But now it became clear to her that his injury, how it had happened and its effect on his life, had been in a sense the elephant in the living room: an unspoken subject that everyone pretended hadn't had an impact—or didn't affect them still.

And if tonight's episode made one thing abundantly clear it was that she herself had made ignoring Griff's accident and its effect second nature—even though the evidence had been right in front of her eyes every day.

To her horror, her eyes filled with tears, and Julia lowered her chin, batting her eyes madly to keep them from falling.

"I'm sorry, Griff," she whispered, mindful that nearly every eye in the room was on the two of them. "I didn't know."

"Know what?" he asked, low, and she could tell from the pitch of his voice that he was more angry than ever. "That I might've been able to dance perfectly well even if I've never done it before? Or that I might want to but didn't relish askin' a woman to have a go at it with me with a bunch of people lookin' on?"

She lifted her chin, letting every bit of her feelings show on her face. "*I* would have!" she vowed fiercely. "Even with hundreds of people looking on!"

"Durn it, Julia, I don't want your pity," he said harshly. "I never have, and I never will."

"Pity!" She stared at him in shock. "How

could you think I'd do anything for you out of pity?"

That seemed to give him pause, but only for a second. "All right, maybe it's not pity. But I sure as hell don't need to be one of the walking wounded you feel you have to champion at every turn."

What he meant by that, she hadn't a clue. But it was clear he had no intention of elaborating.

The song ended and he released her.

Who knew how long they'd have stood there in mute discord if Michele hadn't come shyly forward. "Griff, you've got to forgive me for not knowin' about your accident," she said sincerely.

He turned to her almost absently. "Don't worry about it another minute," he said, and after a moment belatedly treated her to a half smile that was striking mostly in how it was miles different from how he'd just looked at Julia. "You couldn't've known."

Michele smiled her relief. "Well, it's clear it doesn't affect your dancin' a bit. You're as fine a dancer as any cowboy I've ever seen."

Herm had started the tape again, and when the next song, another slow one, began, she asked, "Would you dance one with me? This

George Strait song is one of my all-time favorites."

"It'd be my pleasure."

Julia could only step aside as Griff wheeled Michele away. Unable to watch the two of them, she turned suddenly and almost bowled over Griff's mother, who had come up beside her and was now gazing at her with that soft, motherly gaze she knew so well.

Its compassion made her once again unable to dissemble. "I've been to a hundred dances where Griff was there, and I never thought that he might like to join in," Julia choked.

"Don't beat up on yourself, dear. He's my son and I love him, but he hides his feelings so well that even if he had a passion for something, it'd barely register on anyone's radar."

"But I'm his best friend!" Julia said fiercely. "And I was there when that bull gored him. I saw what it did to him."

Frannie's eyes squeezed shut briefly, as if she herself were trying to banish the picture, even if it could only be imagined, from her mind. "It was a frightening accident. No one judges you for dealing with it however you had to. Neither should any of us judge Griff for dealing with it however he's had to."

She reached out and gave Julia's arm a

squeeze, and Julia managed a smile in return. It helped to have Frannie's understanding.

But she knew her conscience wouldn't rest easy until she had Griff's.

Chapter Five

Julia walked slowly up the darkened, deserted street, the lights in the houses on either side giving her a peek at the lives within them: a man sitting in his easy chair, reading the newspaper; a wife letting the dog in for the night; children in pajamas racing up the front stairs to bed.

She watched them all with the same sense of looking upon the world with new eyes that she'd felt since she'd watched Griff squire Michele around the floor earlier that evening to the music of the different bands. As it happened, it had been the first group the committee listened to—that being the Alamo Gang out of Austin—that was chosen to play at Reb's homecoming celebration.

All thoughts of celebrations and music left her head as Julia stopped at the front gate of one home. There were no lights on here, at least not in the front of the house, which was shrouded in darkness.

Disappointment and relief mingled in her breast.

She tucked her hands into her fleece vest to keep them warm. It was chilly out this evening but not uncomfortably so. The coldest weather wouldn't hit till January, and even then it wasn't truly cold, not in this part of Texas. Still, she didn't look forward to winter, and this one in particular.

She wasn't one to spend her time in the past, but right now she wished she could go back a few weeks to when she'd received that letter from Reb. Heck, if she were wishing, she might as well go back to Griff's accident and somehow keep it from happening. Her heart ached for him and the pain he'd endured then and ever since. Pain she could now see he'd kept carefully inside.

Pain she had, for whatever reason, looked past and ignored.

"Hey, Teach."

She whirled in sheer terror and found a familiar silhouette standing on the sidewalk not ten feet from her.

"Griff!" she exclaimed in surprise, her disappointment turning to apprehension. Certainly she'd come here to talk to him about what had happened at the meeting, but his reaction had been so…emotional. So unlike him, it had startled her as much as he had just now. "You scared me, sneaking up on me like that."

"Like I could sneak up on anyone," he remarked without a bit of self-consciousness. "A peg-legged pirate would have more luck at that than me." He gave a tilt of his head toward his house. "Comin' in?"

"S-sure."

He reached around her to open the gate from the inside, and she preceded him through it and they walked to the front porch, terribly conscious of that catch in his stride that she knew now she'd never again be able to overlook.

She couldn't make out what was going through his head, other than it was the second time that evening he'd referred openly to his limp. She had to wonder what had changed. Had it been Michele engagingly accepting, if not completely discounting, the fact that he had a slight physical limitation? Or was it that he'd been able to deal with one of its effects on his life in an open and matter-of-fact manner?

"I was afraid you had already gone to bed," she said as they climbed the steps to the porch.

"I walked Michele to her aunt's," he said in brief explanation.

"Oh!" she said inanely. Hastily she took a seat on the wooden swing as he leaned against one of the porch columns, waiting expectantly.

"You and she sure seemed to hit it off pretty well," Julia blurted.

He shrugged. "She seems nice. I offered to introduce her to my cousin Lara at the medical clinic. Alma's right in that the clinic could use another nurse."

His mood puzzled her. There was none of the anger coming from him that she'd sensed before, yet he wasn't quite himself, either.

"It sounds as if Bridgewater might be the place for Michele to settle, after all. I'm sure it'll help to know you, too," Julia said sincerely, although she couldn't quite banish the twinges of jealousy that beset in her at the image of the two of them sharing that special moment on the dance floor.

She must, however. She honestly wanted Griff to be happy, wanted him to do what was best for him. Wanted him to find the love he deserved with a woman who would appreciate him for the wonderful, supportive man that he was.

Then why was she feeling so unhappy at the thought of him finding that love with Michele?

"Julia."

She glanced up and realized from the look on Griff's face that he had been talking and she hadn't heard a word.

"I'm sorry, Griff," she apologized. "Did you say something?"

"I just wondered if there was a reason you'd come by."

"Yes." She took a deep breath, figuring she'd get no better opening. "I came by to apologize for being the cause of that awkward moment, with my suggestion about slow dancing. I'm ashamed to say it had never occurred to me that you might feel the lack of taking a girl for a spin around the dance floor," she joked feebly.

It didn't come off in the way she intended. Her voice even gave a little wobble.

Griff obviously heard it, for he took the remaining steps across the porch and settled next to her on the swing. His closeness was both comforting and disturbing to her.

"Julia, why would you feel ashamed about that?" he asked, and it was with that gentle inquiry that she had missed so much. Warmth, where a moment before there'd been emptiness, spread through her chest.

"It's hard to explain." She hesitated, biting her lip. She wanted to pour out to him her regrets about his accident, about having to give up his dreams. About him having to watch Reb live them out. However, such revelations, she was sure, came under the category of—Subjects They'd Agreed Not To Discuss.

So what *could* she say that would let Griff know she understood, even without her saying?

The solution came to her in a flash of intuition. Of course. What was the one subject she *had* found it hard to relate to others?

"You know, Griff, I've never talked to you about my time in Central America, teaching children there," she said.

"That you haven't," he admitted. If he was puzzled by her choice of topic, he didn't show it. "But I figured you would when you could."

She nodded. That made sense.

"It was the most rewarding I've ever spent—and the most difficult," she revealed, although it wasn't easy. There were reasons she hadn't talked about her experience.

"How's that?" he asked, again with that gentle inquiry.

"The kind of poverty...that kind of soul-deep pain for another's pain..." she said haltingly, achingly aware that he had stretched his arm behind her along the back of the swing. "It changes you in ways you don't always realize right away—or even years later. It makes you cautious to realize how fragile your existence is. At the same time it makes you want to risk everything to stay right there in that state of being where you're dealing with what matters most in this world and nothing else. Where you're most alive."

She shook her head slowly, concentrating, almost trying to will herself back to that kind of state. "But it's impossible to stay there, to stay in the moment," she said out loud. "I don't know why, but it is. Maybe we're not meant to, as human beings. You know what I mean?"

"Yeah," he answered thoughtfully. "Yeah, I think I do. It's not only hard to stay in that place, but hard to get to. A lot of doubts and fears get in the way. I think you're right, though, and we're not equipped to stay in the moment every second. But I do think we're meant to try, 'cause that's what makes life worth livin'."

Surprised, Julia glanced over at him, wondering that she hadn't confided these thoughts to Griff before, for it was clear that he did understand.

She was no longer chilly, but warm— warmed by the connection with Griff that she'd always had with him, except she felt it now more than ever.

It made her want to maintain the honesty of the moment. "You know, I joined the Peace Corps to make a difference, of course—but I also went away for personal reasons."

He shifted on the seat next to her, and the movement caused the swing to sway slightly. "Such as?" he asked.

"By that time, Reb had asked me to marry him. Several times. And I was trying to figure out whether I wanted to marry him. If that was right for me." She stopped. "I'm sorry, Griff. I forgot that I'm not to go there with you."

He actually moved closer still. "True—but I think that's dependent on what you're tryin' to figure out right now."

She met his gaze squarely. "And I guess

that is, I couldn't appreciate it until I'd gone to Central America the kind of life-changing experience it must have been for you when you were in that accident. Especially afterward. Even if I'd been able to fully appreciate it, I don't think I was able to express it to you then, at fifteen. Or to comprehend the strength of character it had taken for *you* at fifteen to pull yourself up, pull yourself through. Even if you hardly showed it to me, it must have been incredibly hard, because I'd never really realized until this evening..."

Her voice trailed off as she lost the gist of her point and how this was related to her feeling for Reb, although she couldn't have said why. So she finished, somewhat lamely but sincerely, "I never realized I hadn't told you how much I've always admired that about you."

She took his hand, so glad to feel easy in doing so. So glad her best friend was here and they were free to talk about their deepest secrets and fears.

Apparently, though, she was the only one who felt that way.

"It seems to me, actually, that you haven't ignored what happened all these years," Griff said. He pulled his hand away, sitting back.

"You just didn't deal with it. You still haven't dealt with it. Dealt with me."

"Griff!" She was shocked, again by this polar shift in his mood. "What do you mean?"

He stared at her, and she wondered desperately what reassurance he was searching for in her eyes that he couldn't seem to find. Finally he turned away, obviously unsatisfied. Obviously disappointed.

She wouldn't let him do it, not this time. She grasped his arm and wouldn't let herself be shaken off. "No, Griff, don't. Don't turn away. Don't hide your feelings from me. You do that, you know. All the time. And I've learned to accept that as your choice or your nature or whatever the situation may be. But don't do it now, please. I do want to know."

In profile, he looked about as torn as a man could be. Torn about what?

"Please," she whispered.

Still he said nothing, for several beats of her heart. She could see his strong jaw bulging with effort, and twice his Adam's apple bobbed as he swallowed painfully. What *was* it he hid from her?

Or what was it he doubted she could understand or accept about him?

Pushing herself to her knees on the swing,

she reached out to place her hand on his cheek and turn his face toward her so that she could look him in the eye, could put everything in her heart in her own eyes.

"Tell me, Griff," she pleaded, her voice cracking. "We're friends. Best friends. Remember what you said to me? Nothing you could say or do could ever change that. Whatever you are, whatever you feel, I could never consider it wrong. I'd never turn away from it. I promise you."

Again he scrutinized her, hard, his gaze delving into hers as if he had been stranded on a desert island for years, and hers was the first face, the first voice, he'd encountered in all that time. And apparently this time he found what he searched for.

Because then, slowly, he took her wrist—and pressed her palm to his thigh.

Through the taut denim she could feel the rock-hard cast of muscle. Could feel, too, as he dragged her hand along his thigh, the furrow that ran the length of that muscle, a furrow that had been carved by the knife-sharp horn with the thrust of a ton of bull behind it.

Abruptly she was back in that dusty corral, sitting on the fence, helplessly watching her two best friends in danger. Feeling her world stop on its axis as Griff took that horrible hit…

Confusion assaulted her and Julia automatically pulled her hand away as if burned, a move she immediately regretted to her soul when she saw hurt and disappointment flash across Griff's features before he could hide them.

Tears sprang to her eyes.

"Griff, I'm sorry!" she cried. "I didn't mean… It's not that I'm repelled by you, by what you—it could never be that! I just…"

Completely stricken, she let her voice trail off, unable to explain.

His mouth tightened into a thin line. Then, as if by that strength of will she'd just praised, it eased and softened.

"It's all right, Julia," he said, although she could tell it was not. His voice was hoarse from strain. "If anything, I'm the one who needs to apologize, for concentratin' on my selfish concerns when you're tied in knots over this thing with Reb. I shouldn't have pressed you, but I thought, when you said you had to go away to decide about Reb and you, that the reason was…was because…"

He shook his head. "I don't know what I thought."

But some instinct about him told her he *did* think something and *still* was choosing not to say it. Still believed she could not understand.

She must show him she could!

"Yes, I did go away to figure things out about Reb and me," she said as, her hand shaking, she once more set her palm upon Griff's thigh, feeling for the ridged furrow there. "I wasn't sure then…and it almost seems as if it's for the same reasons I'm not certain now."

"Which are?" he asked in a strained voice.

But she didn't answer him. Couldn't answer him, as she closed her eyes in an effort to let herself experience the moment when he'd sustained that injury, this time not shying away from her own pain. Her own horror as she'd watched him fly through the air and land, his body as limp as his face was contorted in agony, for in that moment her life had changed, as well.

That was what she had meant to tell him a moment ago: that she had nearly lost the person she loved most in the world, and it had scared her to death. Scared her away from letting her feel that love to its fullest depth.

For she did—she loved Griff. She had always loved him.

Her eyes shot open. *But...but you love Reb that way!* the voice in Julia's head screamed at her. *Not Griff.* Reb was the man she was going to marry.

Griff, however, is the man you're meant to love, whispered her heart.

"Julia?" Griff said, and the single word thrummed with urgent inquiry.

Julia rose in a rush. She couldn't let him know. She needed to get out of here, needed to get to her own home where she could be alone and sort this whole tangled mess out, before she said or did something that could not be taken back, that would affect her friendship with Griff.

But the force of her haste propelled the swing backward, and on its sweep forward it hit her in the back of the knees, making her stumble. She landed hard, her knee digging into Griff's injured thigh.

Her gaze flew to his as his hands gripped her waist, her own hands instinctively going to support her body by spreading on his solid, wide chest. For the second time in a minute she saw the pain she caused him in those violet-blue eyes. Eyes she knew as well as her own, and what she saw there both shocked her and brought her ease.

For his pain wasn't physical. It beat from his heart, its timbre coming to her through bone and sinew to vibrate under her palms.

"Did you never wonder why *I* went away?" he whispered, his mouth only a breath from hers.

She started to shake her head no when, in preternatural flash, the answer to both his questions, what he'd wanted her to know in touching him, came to her: *he* loved *her*. Had always loved her, and would have spoken his love that fateful day had he not rushed to the aid of his best friend.

The tension of it in him was palpable, drawn in every line of his face, along with the pain. And despite her fears and doubts, she would not turn away from it. Couldn't, no matter the consequences.

The moment held, and it was like a dream, one she'd thought would never come true.

Then he was kissing her. No—that was too mild an expression for the way their lips melded together as one. His mouth was familiar and strange at once, like that dream where everything doesn't make sense while still making perfect sense. The way he slid his hands up to cup her face and bring her closer still was a complement to her own will and want to be one with him. She curled her fingers against his chest like a cat, and he groaned back in his throat, his kiss growing even wilder and deeper, until it became too much to bear, and they both broke contact to drag in huge drafts of air.

"I love you, Julia," he rasped against her throat. "I can't keep it inside me anymore."

"I know, I know," she whispered back. "I love you, too."

His head came up at that so that he could peer at her with the kind of scrutiny, the kind of reverence, usually reserved for the revelation of miracles.

"You...you do?" he asked, his voice thick with emotion, doubt warring with hope.

She nodded slowly. "I never knew it until now, but yes, I love you."

Oh, the thrill that charged through her at the look of such deep satisfaction, of deep intimacy, in those wonderfully expressive eyes!

Now it was she who tugged on his collar to bring him close to kiss him again. His hands were as fervent as his mouth, grazing first down the outside of her hip to her thigh, then upward again to her rib cage to circle the undersides of her breasts. Julia gasped at the pleasure she'd never experienced so completely before, and he took her open mouth to his.

She'd never known Griff to be so passionate, so unrestrained. So in and of the moment as they'd just talked about. Knowing him so made her feel as alive as she'd ever felt: glorious, completely fulfilling, while as frightening as jumping off a cliff. He'd always been the calm one among the three friends, the one to provide gentle restraint when her zealousness to right every wrong in the world threatened to gallop out of control. Had always been the steadying influence on Reb's own brand of impulsiveness that lived, if anything, too much in the moment and without caution…

Reb.

With a cry, Julia tore her mouth from Griff's.

"What are we doing?" she asked, horrified. Realizing she lay half prone across his body, she leapt to her feet, which sent the swing rocking again.

She pressed her hands to her cheeks. They were burning. Burning in shame. *"What are we doing?"*

"Julia," Griff said, low, reaching for her again. Whether it was to comfort or to pull her back into his embrace, she didn't know, but she couldn't go there again, for she knew which outcome she wanted.

"Griff, how could you?" she cried, stepping back. Her action brought hurt to his eyes and made every bit of her part in letting this happen bear down on her like a locomotive.

"How could *I?*" he said with a lift of his eyebrows.

"All right! How can *we* do this to Reb?"

"And just what is 'this'?" he asked obtusely, although his eyes, even in the dim light, seemed as sharply defined and astute as a jungle cat's.

"This!" she cried nonsensically, gesturing between them. "Kissing each other, feeling these feelings—"

"Feelings such as loving each other enough that we'd both completely forget anything and anyone else in the world—"

"Stop it!" Her voice shook. "You know what I mean."

"Yes, Julia, I do." He pushed himself to his feet, although he didn't approach her, thank goodness. "And I can't say I'm sorry that things are finally out in the open."

"Finally? How long have *you* known?" she demanded, crossing her arms defensively. She felt at a distinct disadvantage here, as if she needed to play catch-up with her own heart.

"Known that I loved you?" Griff said. "Since I was old enough to recognize those kinds of feelings. You've always been the only one for me, Julia."

For some reason that made anger boil up in her. "You mean you *knew* you loved me and you didn't tell me?"

"That's right," he returned with the same equanimity that made her almost believe he hadn't been wild for her just a few moments ago. "I knew when you and Reb started dating. I knew when you were trying to decide whether to marry Reb. Knew when you got engaged and I went away to try and deal with that fact—that I loved you."

"And you couldn't have mentioned this when I might have had a choice in the matter?" she asked, quite illogically.

"That was the problem. You would've had to choose, and I couldn't have done that to you any more than I'd have done it to Reb."

He leaned negligently against one of the porch columns. "Besides, you'd already made your choice—twice. Once when I got out of the hospital and came back to school to discover my two best friends were goin' steady, the other when you came back from the Peace Corps."

"Oh, so now it's my fault?" Again she knew she sounded as illogical as rain during a snowstorm, but she couldn't seem to help herself. And that scared her even more.

"No," he said almost regretfully. "That's the other thing, Julia. When people fall in love, it's not anyone's fault."

He was right. She gave a huff of pure frustration. Pure misery. Here she was with Griff, whom she did love as no one else, knew he loved her so, as well, and it was awful. *Awful.*

"Well, it's still wrong to act on these feelings," she repeated defiantly. "I'm engaged to Reb. I know it sounds impossible, but I *love* Reb, too."

"Even though he's the one thinking of calling off your engagement?" Griff asked. He was definitely back to that calm, cool, impenetrable demeanor of his. She hated it, especially now that she knew what he hid beneath its surface.

"Yes!" she retorted. "Who knows how that situation will end up? But until it's resolved, I can't betray his trust."

Her own words struck a chord in her, and she covered her mouth with her hand in horror. "Griff, did you know already that I had these feelings for *you?* Is that what you meant when you said you wouldn't let me betray Reb after that…that accidental kiss?"

"I suspected that there were feelings on your side, yes," he admitted slowly, seeming to gauge her reaction. "That's what made things so frustrating—what kept me from saying anything, in case I was wrong."

"But how?" She registered how distraught she sounded. "How could you know what I didn't know myself?"

"Maybe deep down you knew, and you didn't want to deal with it, like you didn't want to deal with me and my accident."

"Or maybe because I knew it wasn't right!" she corrected, pointing at him.

For an unholy dread of some portentous event had certainly taken hold in her.

Now Griff did take those steps toward her, and she very nearly panicked that he'd touch her again and prove her a liar.

Yet when he stopped in front of her, his arms remained at his sides while hers hugged her middle tightly.

"You said that whatever I feel or do or am couldn't be wrong, not in your eyes," he demanded. "So are you saying now that my loving you—and your loving me—is wrong?"

"No!" she cried.

"Then were you saying that once Reb comes back, and you and he break it off," he pressed, "*then* it'll be right for us to love each other?"

"No!" She shook her head, more confused than she'd ever been in her life.

Pivoting away from him, she blindly stumbled to one side of the porch. She clutched the cold hard railing with both hands, praying for direction. She wanted desperately to get away from him before the situation deteriorated even further—before their friendship was torn completely asunder, never to be repaired. Surely it couldn't be, though. She and Griff were too good friends to let anything come between them.

As confused as she was, however, she had the wherewithal to understand that after tonight, nothing in the three of their lives would ever be the same again.

"Oh, what will we do, Griff?" she whispered, unable to keep herself from reaching out to him yet again, as she always had. "What will we do?"

She heard him sigh heavily. "I don't know that it's up to me what happens next, Julia."

Yes. She had accused him of taking away her choices, and now she had one. She must not make the wrong one—wrong for her.

She lifted her chin. "Well, Reb and I still have to talk out whatever doubts he's feeling and decide what to do. Who knows how our friendship will be affected, but I simply can't think about that right now." Her throat clogged with tears again at the mere thought.

He came up behind her, and it took everything in her power not to turn into the circle of his arms. "I know Reb, Julia. He's not going to cut you out of his life even if the two of you aren't meant to be," Griff said gently. "I mean, I wouldn't do that. I couldn't."

Finally he did put his hands on her shoulders, and she found herself moving away from his touch almost defensively.

When she reached the corner of the porch, she turned to face him. Made herself look him in the eye.

"I hope you mean that, Griff," she told him. "Because…because as for the two of us— maybe that's not meant to be, either."

Chapter Six

Griff had thought he'd experienced just about his limit this evening as far as extremes of emotion, but he'd obviously been wrong, as euphoria plummeted into another abyss of discouragement.

Still, he managed to hold on to one bouying thought—that at last he had spoken, and at last Julia knew that he loved her. And she *loved* him!

He let himself feel a brief moment of vindication at least on that point. Damn it, he'd known that Julia loved him in that way, and not Reb. He'd *known* it, ever since forever.

So you're right. Where does that get you?

Yes, it was small comfort, considering how she apparently saw no hope right now for a future together.

Please—don't let me lose her now that I finally have her, he prayed. That would be the worst luck yet!

"But you and I, we do love each other," he said almost desperately. "I know I've always loved you, and I always knew deep down that you loved me that way, too. And you don't think we're meant to be? Why?"

"Don't you see? Who knows what will happen between Reb and me if we decide to break off our engagement?" She looked so unhappy it made his gut twist, because the fact of the matter was, he was the direct cause of that unhappiness. "I think that's what was worrying me more these past weeks than wondering if he had doubts about our relationship. Even if the break is mutual, Griff, things *will* never be the same. Sure, we may still be friends, but it's like I said—we can't go back to the way it was before."

She closed her eyes as if in dire pain. "That's why we can't let these feelings between the two of *us* go anywhere. It's because we're best friends, and I can't—won't—risk losing you as a friend, too. And once we started that kind of relationship, that possibility would become very, very real."

She opened her eyes to look at him intently. "Is that why you never spoke?"

He couldn't lie to her. "Not exactly. I wasn't thinkin' of our friendship, but the one I had with Reb. I knew that to speak my piece would pit the two of us against each other. You'd have to choose, and if it wasn't Reb…I didn't want to lose Reb as a friend. Because I knew he loved you, too."

Her mouth trembled. "So you know I'm right in believing there's that risk…between us."

He looked away, not answering her. He couldn't lie to her.

Blast it, he should have kept his mouth shut, should have let her continue to search for a reason why it just didn't feel "right," until the answer dawned on her. He knew Julia well enough to have figured out she'd never have gone through with the wedding, not with even one doubt about her and Reb's relationship.

If he had just *waited* until she'd come to that conclusion on her own! But tonight he had realized that he might have waited too long already. He'd had to admit to Julia and the whole durned town practically that he had never tried dancing with a woman. Had never taken even that small of a risk. The lack had seemed to characterize the very substance of his life. And so it would have killed him to stand by and say nothing yet again.

"Look, Julia, it's inevitable," he tried again. "Friendships change. Relationships change. But change isn't a bad thing, not all the time, and for sure not if things need to change."

"That may be true. I hope to heaven Reb and I can be best friends again—still." She bit her lower lip, her gaze downcast. "But with you, Griff... Somehow I know it'd be different with you if, once we crossed over that line between friends and...and lovers, and things didn't work out between us... I would die if I lost you as a friend, Griff. I can't risk it."

Risk. There was that word again, like a thorn in his side. "But they *will* work out. How could they not? We *love* each other."

The evening had only grown colder as they'd talked, and he reached out to take her arm again, thinking that the physical contact would at least keep them connecting as they hashed this matter out, because he could sense that he was indeed losing her.

Yet she evaded his touch again, and it raised every kind of fear in him, even as she said, "Reb and I believed that about each other, too. Believed it for almost ten years. Please, try to understand. That's a long time not to know your own heart, Griff. That's why I can't risk discovering what else my heart is hiding in that kind of relationship with you."

"Yet you were willing to risk it with Reb," he pointed out, and not in the nicest manner, either.

That seemed to stop her. Then she said softly, "Actually, *Reb* was willing to risk it, while you made a choice, too—not to speak, not to act."

Oh, but that cut deep! To the very bone. And he knew then that, despite everything, he was losing again. Losing Julia, when he barely had a moment to savor the sweetness of knowing her love.

It seemed impossible, unnatural. And yet he could see in her hazel eyes that she would stand firm on this, with that conviction of spirit he had so admired in her.

"Well, if I didn't act," he finally said, "it was because I didn't want to lose the two best friends I'd ever have, either," he returned, now deadly calm. "And in spite of everything, I still don't."

He crammed his fingers into the front pockets of his jeans, partially because they'd froze and partly to keep from reaching for her one more time, just to prove her wrong.

But he'd taken that chance tonight, and look where it had gotten him.

"So I guess it's back to business as usual for me," he went on with a biting tone. If he'd ever wondered if he had a boiling point, he was for sure experiencing it now. "I'm damned if I do, damned if I don't. Well, you can count on me not doing a durned thing to make things work out between us, since that's what you obviously prefer!"

Bitter—that was how he sounded. Bitter as bile. Bitter in a way he hadn't felt when he'd had cause to, with Reb moving in on Julia while he was laid up in the hospital after saving his best friend's life.

At the realization, desolation swept through Griff like a desert wind. He did not want to be this way: bitter and angry and resentful. He had made the conscious decision ten years ago not to give himself over to such a negative attitude, and he'd managed to live up to that decision.

But now…now there was so much more at stake. So much more to lose.

He glanced up to see the same realization had struck Julia—that, in fact, her worst fear would come true, despite everything, and their friendship was already changing.

"I—I'm sorry, Griff," she said, turning and stumbling down the porch steps, nearly running down the sidewalk to her home a few blocks away.

He did not go after her, but peered after her retreating form until it was the merest of shadows in the night and his eyes were stinging with the effort.

Then Griff turned and slammed the heel of his hand into the wood column on his front porch.

Pain reverberated up his arm and into his shoulder, making him gasp. But it was pain he welcomed, for as those years before, it helped distract him from the gash that had been torn through his heart.

JULIA PUT THE finishing touch on the last present she had to wrap with a desultory air. Christmas day was only two days away, and her holiday mood had turned distinctly Grinchy.

"Is it safe to come in here yet?" her father asked, peeking around the doorjamb.

"Oh. Yes, I'm done," she answered, gathering together the spools of bright ribbon and rolls of wrapping paper on the kitchen table. The reds, greens, silvers and golds were such a contrast to her mood, she involuntarily sighed.

Andy Sennett apparently misread the reason for her sigh, for he commented, "You always get the lion's share of responsibility for decorating and wrapping around holiday time, don't you, daughter? Kinda takes the merriness out of it if it's an obligation."

"I don't mind."

He affectionately cuffed a hand around the back of her neck. "Since you're done, come watch the Cowboys' game with me. You haven't told me how much you despise my favorite football team in a modern age. I never thought I'd say this, but I've missed you lording it over me ever' time the 'Boys get scored against."

He added coaxingly, "They're down by six, as we speak."

Julia brightened at the prospect. Spending the afternoon with her father was just what she needed to get out of her funk. Later, she'd whip up a pot of chili and some Texas toast for supper. Maybe they'd even put up a few Christmas decorations, although they were about as late as one could be without actually sitting on top of the holiday itself.

"Let me make a batch of popcorn and I'll be in," she volunteered.

Fifteen minutes later, Julia sat cross-legged on the sofa with a bowl of popcorn settled in her lap as she cheered for the Arizona Cardinals, effectively pitting Sennett against Sennett.

The Cards were making a fine hash of the 'Boys, much to Andy's consuming disgust. When the phone rang halfway through the third quarter, he reached for it on the side table even as he bemoaned, "Wouldya look at that? The ball slipped clean through his fingers!"

He barked into the receiver, "Hello!" only to have his whole expression soften instantly. "Well, hey there, you. No, no. Just watchin' Dallas get the stuffin' kicked out of 'em. You're a welcome diversion, that's for sure."

Who was on the other end of the line that could make her father's eyes brighten so noticeably? Julia wondered. Definitely someone of the female persuasion, she guessed as she watched in fascination as Andy threw back his head on a hearty laugh.

"Dang if you don't know me!" he exclaimed, then listened intently. "Why, that'd be great. I appreciate it... Now, there's an idea. I'd love to… Okeydoke, see you later, then. 'Bye."

Julia let a full five minutes go by before she had to ask, "Who was that on the phone, Dad?"

"Oh, that was Frannie Corbin," he answered readily, his gaze never leaving the television screen.

In her astonishment, Julia dropped a handful of kernels down the front of her sweatshirt. "Griff's mom?"

"Yup. She wanted to know if she could make the dish our family's to contribute to the gathering at the Farleys's on Christmas day." He shot her a quick confirming glance. "She figured you've been pretty tied up with Reb's big homecomin' do, and she knows I can't cook worth a lick."

He grabbed a handful of popcorn and tipped his head back to toss it into his mouth. Chewing, he added, "I'm going over there after the game to lend her a hand."

Her own troubles fell to the wayside as Julia gazed at her father with new eyes. Andy Sennett was a barrel-chested man of fifty, and a widower for twenty of those years. She knew he'd had a few romances over time, but none of the women had ever seemed to make him perk up like Griff's mother did.

Finally she had to ask. "So…is there something going on between the two of you?"

Still he stared at the brightly lit screen, although his eyes mellowed. "She's a fine woman, Frannie is. Between you and me, I care about her more and more every day, it seems."

Incredulity made her tease impulsively, "Do I hear wedding bells?" She immediately regretted her joke, however, at the serious cast that came over her father's face as he finally looked at her.

"Web Corbin was one of my best friends," he said. "Both he and Frannie stood 'side me after your mother died when you were just a little girl."

"You don't need to tell me, Dad," Julia said, abashed. "I don't think a week has gone by in twenty years when someone in the Corbin family hasn't stopped by to bring one of Frannie's pies or a casserole, or to invite you, Ty or me to some activity, even if it's just to go the next town over to see a movie."

Andy nodded. "Then you can see why, even if I do find myself carin' for Frannie more 'n' more each day, it's not somethin' that might ever be right to act on. There's too much history, too many feelings of a different nature that've passed between us."

In shock, Julia set her popcorn bowl aside. Her father could have been speaking about herself and Griff.

"But...couldn't it be that from such feelings come the best and deepest relationships?" She leaned forward on her elbows. "I mean, when you know someone inside and out, wouldn't it make sense that you already have a start on something deep and lasting?"

She must have sounded pretty urgent for her father put his arm around her shoulders and gave them a squeeze. "Darlin', I wasn't talkin' about you and Reb. Not at all. Of course you can fall in love with your best friend. But there's a difference between that and falling in love with the woman your best friend was married to and made a life with."

She stared at her lap, hoping he wouldn't see the tears that burned her eyes. She'd thought she hadn't any left to cry.

So it seemed she was not meant to escape her troubles today. But then, how could she escape what was so much a part of her—her love for Griff?

"Are you sure you're okay, daughter?"

Andy asked, dipping his chin to peer into her face.

Julia shifted, uncrossing her legs and not answering. She found it utterly ironic that had the situation not concerned Frannie's son, Julia herself would have talked things over with the older woman. For that matter, she'd have talked things over with Griff!

She missed him, terribly. Not in the sense of time or space. It had only been a few days since those glorious stolen moments on his porch swing, and it wasn't as if he weren't a mere few blocks away. Within shouting distance, practically. No, she missed what they'd had together, what they'd been to each other that she was afraid could never be completely recaptured, even now. He was her best friend, the one person she knew best, who knew her best. Who loved her as she loved him.

She pressed her lips together, stifling a sob.

"There *is* somethin' wrong, Julia," Andy said. He tugged her closer, till her head was on his shoulder in that pose that fathers and daughters had both drawn comfort from through the ages. "Won't you tell me?"

"Daddy, I would if I thought it was something that could be helped by talking about it, honestly." She sighed. "But I think I need to figure this out on my own."

"Is it Reb?" Her father's breath ruffled her hair. "You know I think the world of that boy, but marriage to him will take a lot of patience and sacrifice."

She fiddled with the sleeve of his Western shirt, pleating the material. "Why do you think that, Daddy?"

"Every marriage takes those two qualities, of course. Reb, though…he's always seemed the impulsive type to me, which is his strength in the rodeo ring." He shifted, pulling her closer. "I'm no expert on ridin' bulls, but you've got to be able to rid yourself of the fears of past bust-ups and breaks, while not anticipatin' the buzzer at the end of those eight seconds, and just go with the moment of what that bull's gonna do. But too much livin' your life that way is hard on those around you. There's consequences."

What did her father mean? "Do you think Reb can't be consistent and stick to a goal?" she asked almost defensively, immediately wondering why she was so. "He can, though. He's spent the last nine years workin' toward becoming a champion bull rider."

"Sure, he's proven he can go the distance

on the bulls. But a marriage is different. There, he'll have to prove he can go the distance with you."

Julia bit down so hard on her bottom lip she wondered if she'd drawn blood. But she had to say it. "Dad, what if it's not Reb but me who can't go the distance?"

"You?" Her father's arm tightened around her. "You're nowhere the kind of person who tucks tail at adversity, darlin'. Why, look how you went to Central America and taught those little ones. Look at how you're always takin' on one cause after another."

It was good to have her father's faith in her, but she knew she had to be scrupulously honest. "Sure, but that's not the kind of test that you face in a marriage. Marriage takes a whole lot more…being able, like you said, to rid yourself of the fears of past bust-ups and breaks and disasters—and letting yourself love someone to the fullest."

Andy thought on that for a while before answering. "Well, you never get rid of those fears, I'll say that first. So you just learn to love in spite of 'em—or you learn to love because of 'em." He kissed the top of her head. "And believe me, Julia, you're not the type to let such fears, whatever they might be, hold you hostage forever. I've always admired that in you."

Julia sighed, pressing her cheek to her father's shoulder. She was as confused as ever, but it helped to have Andy's faith in her that she'd do the right thing.

She just wished she knew what that was.

"You know," she murmured, "I told Griff something similar the other evening. That I admired him for not letting his injury hold him back or turn him bitter—"

Except he *had* sounded bitter, incredibly so. And it had been because what had been an unvoiced possibility for so many years had become an impossible reality.

She died inside every time it hit her that she had played a part in that transformation.

On that thought, Julia sat forward and out of the circle of her father's comforting embrace, her back to him. He apparently saw nothing amiss in the action, for he said musingly, "You know, there once was a time when I thought, rather than you and Reb, that maybe…"

It took all of her will not to whirl and stare at him. "When you thought what, Dad?"

But he only clicked his tongue. "Nah. There's nothing to be gained in speculatin' on what might've been. Such as if your mama had lived and got to see you married to Reb Farley." He gave a chuckle. "You know, she told me a story once about how, when she saw you, Reb and Griff lined up next to each other in the hospital nursery, she'd known your lives were destined to be twined together some way."

Now Julia did turn to face her father, whose eyebrows had knit over his brown eyes. "I mean, it was clear even before she passed on that the three of you were thick as thieves. But she told me something else…something about you and one of the boys set up side by side like a little bride and groom, and the other boy's bassinet getting wedged between y'all, which made you start cryin' something fierce."

"Was it Reb or Griff that came between us?" she asked, her heart in her throat. Oh, perhaps the guidance or sign or whatever she'd unconsciously asked for had come!

"For the life of me, I can't recall." He lifted his shoulders, then let them fall. "Well, it doesn't matter now, does it? You're set to marry Reb Farley soon."

He clapped his hand on his knee. "Say, why don't you come on over to the Corbins' with me when I go? Frannie'd love to have your help. And come to think of it, she might know the full of that story about you three friends as babies. I'm pretty sure both she and Sue Farley were there when it happened."

Julia thought for a moment, then shook her head. "No thanks. I think I'll stay here."

"Suit yourself—aw, no!" Andy leapt to his feet. "Not another interception!"

She was glad her father was back to being engrossed in the game. That way he wouldn't notice just how preoccupied his offer had made her.

Suddenly she wanted nothing less than to know what fate had had in store for herself, Griff and Reb.

Or what it might still have in store for them.

THE FARLEY HOME was bursting with smells of turkey roasting and apple pies baking. Elvis's rendition of "Blue Christmas" wafted toward Julia, along with the inevitable blare of a college football game in progress on the television, to where she stood just on the inside of the threshold.

"Merry Christmas, Sennetts all," Sue Farley greeted the family, with hugs for Julia and her father.

"Where's Ty?" she asked. "I thought you'd persuaded him to leave off that globe-trotting he does for the government to get home for Christmas."

"And would you have the secret to that kind of influence over your own son that you'd let me in on?" Andy Sennett asked with a wink.

"You got me there," Sue returned wryly. She turned to Julia excitedly. "Reb called an hour ago and said he had a meetin' first thing tomorrow mornin' where he expected to seal the deal on a big endorsing contract. For Justin Boots, can you believe that! Anyway, it's all getting signed and sealed in L.A., which I don't understand being as how the boots are made here in Texas."

Her grasp on Julia's arm was meant to comfort. "He said not to worry 'bout him being lonely, that he's having Christmas with his agent's family."

Julia hoped her face didn't show her guilt, but it must have shown some emotion that Reb's mom misinterpreted as disappointment at missing his call.

"Aw, don't you worry now, hon." Sue squeezed her shoulders. "He said to give you a hug from him and to let you know he was anxious to get home and get things settled."

Her eyebrows lifted in anticipation. "Am I right in guessin' that means y'all have got a weddin' date in mind?"

"That's still as much up in the air as it was," Julia said evasively. How on earth was she going to make it through this day keeping up this act that all was well between Reb and her? Without blurting out the truth?

And what was the truth? That she was in love with Griff Corbin? What would that kind of news do to all three of their families?

She could only imagine. Even if she, Reb and Griff *could* work out some solution between them, the ramifications went further than the three of them. Somewhere, there'd be hurt feelings—hard feelings—that would linger and eventually drive a wedge between them all.

She could almost see why Griff had chosen not to speak for all those years. Almost.

"Merry Christmas!" came another shout from the front hall, along with a rush of cold air and a stamping of feet.

Julia turned and spied Griff himself as he came through the front doorway after his mother. And once she'd seen him, she could not look away as her knees threatened to buckle. He wore the familiar Stetson, of course, but today, instead of the typical Wrangler jeans and work shirt, he wore a pair of black wool slacks and a turtleneck sweater in a shade of periwinkle that matched his eyes.

And the look in them when he found her across the room made her knees even weaker.

Heavens, he looked good! How had she gone for a lifetime not recognizing how much she loved him? And how he loved her? No, she admitted in her heart of hearts, she wanted that never to change. Yet she was vitally afraid it would.

For that matter, it already had.

"Hello, Griff," she said with a tremor in her voice as he reached her, having dispensed hugs and handshakes along the way.

"Merry Christmas, Jules," he murmured. There was an awkward moment in which she suffered every manner of silent nerves, and then he engulfed her in one of his comforting hugs.

She squeezed her eyes shut, reveling in the familiar contact, and hugged him back.

Winter stole back into her heart when he let her go.

"Julia, it's so good to see you again!" Lara Dearborn said, skirting around him and giving Julia a friendly hug.

"Good to see you, too, Lara." She was surprised to see Lara here, but then, as Frannie's niece and Griff's cousin, it made sense that she would be invited to share Christmas with the families. "When we last met, I believe you'd just treated one of my students for scrapes she'd gotten climbing through a barbed-wire fence."

Lara tilted her head to one side. "Kelly, wasn't it? How's she doing?"

"Physically, she's fully recovered," Julia answered, then lowered her voice. "Emotionally—there's a boy she likes who's apparently oblivious to her feelings for him."

"Clueless, I'm sure." Lara tsked.

"Who's clueless?" interjected her fiancé, Connor Brody. The tall, good-looking rancher leaned around Lara to give Julia's hand a hearty hello shake.

"When it comes to matters of the heart, you men are, of course," Lara answered patiently.

Connor was Griff's friend as well as his boss at Tanglewood, and although he was discreet, Julia caught the significant glance he threw Griff that told her he knew there were feelings between his ranch manager and her.

Mild alarm beset her. Had Griff told him about what had occurred between the two of them? Yet that wouldn't be Griff at all. If anything, her closed-mouth friend would be even less revealing about something like this. So it likely was that Connor had figured the situation out—and that meant that something in Griff's manner showed.

And if it was apparent to Connor, it would be evident to others—especially Reb.

She was distracted from this worrying thought by Connor himself.

"Well, would you look at that—mistletoe," he said, flourishing a few stems of something green over his fiancée's head. Before she could react, he pulled her to him and took her upturned mouth with his in a stirring kiss. Releasing her a long moment later, Lara, who was blond and fair, turned an attractive shade of pink.

"Connor, honestly!" she admonished him, but her shining eyes belied her tone. "That's not mistletoe, it's a sprig of sage!"

"Whatever," he returned with equanimity, smiling at her intimately as everyone laughed.

They were so evidently in love, so evidently right for each other and secure in that rightness, it brought a surge of longing to Julia's chest. Her gaze met Griff's for only a moment. She had to look away or she was afraid she'd burst into tears. How on earth had things gotten so complicated, so fast?

Things got no less so as the day wore on. She barely tasted her dinner, could hardly concentrate on the animated conversation around her. No one seemed to mind her silence. In fact, at one point Gary Farley gave her a pat on the shoulder and said, "You're missin' your cowboy, aren't you, darlin'? We all are. Well, he'll be home soon and everything'll be set right again, just you wait and see."

"I'll admit I'm anxious to see my boy, too," Sue admitted. "I don't think I'll rest easy till I see him back here, in his own home, where he belongs. All his talk about L.A. and rubbin' elbows with bigwigs—" she glanced around the table with a watery smile "—it sure enough makes me wonder if all this fame has changed him, changed him for good."

"Nothin' could change our Reb," her husband assured her, patting her hand. "Why, don't you think so, too, Griff? You and he are about as close of friends as can be."

Was she the only one who felt the sudden tension in the air of a thousand emotional undercurrents?

Julia saw Griff's throat work as he set a

fork of potatoes back on his plate. "People change, that's a fact of life," he stated simply, without contention. He'd removed his hat, and his wavy black hair fell over his forehead, making him look even more earnest.

His gaze made a tour of the gathering. "Relationships change. They have to, 'cause people grow. They learn new things about the world and about themselves. And before you know it, nothing's the same."

He looked straight at her. "No one's the same, including yourself. And it's not necessarily for the worse."

Oh, there was tension in the air, all right, and it suddenly stretched tighter than a banjo string.

Gary cleared his throat. "Well, I'll wager this winter's wheat crop that our Reb has changed not a lick. And you'll know it for sure, Julia, the minute he gets here and gives you a big kiss!"

There were murmurs of assent as Julia, her heart pounding out of her chest, continued to stare at Griff, and he at her. She knew what he was thinking—of Reb kissing her, and all that that implied.

It struck her only then just how different from Griff it had been for her to kiss Reb.

Intimacy between them had always been… nice. Familiar. Comforting.

As she watched, Griff's eyes darkened dangerously, telling her he knew that intimacy with Reb had not been passionate. Undeniable. Uncontrollable.

As it had been with Griff.

Chapter Seven

Julia rose, her napkin, embroidered with festive holly berries, falling to the carpet.

"W-would you all excuse me, please?" she said hoarsely. "I need to get some air."

"Aw, honey, it *is* Reb, isn't it?" Sue asked, her forehead puckered with concern.

Oh, if you only knew! she wanted to tell her, but only nodded.

"Griff didn't mean what he said." Gary spoke up. "Did you, Griff?"

On the other side of the table, her father started to rise. "Let me take care of this, Gary."

"It's not Griff! *Or* Reb!" she said emphatically. Her palms were damp with perspiration, and she ran them down the front of her slacks. "I—I'm afraid I'm not very good company today. I just need a little time alone, that's all."

With that, she turned and fairly ran for the front door, grabbing her jacket off the coat-rack on her way out.

Once she'd run a few hundred feet down the lane, she felt better. The temperature was only in the forties, but there was a nip in the wind out here in the country where there weren't a lot of sheltering buildings. It stung her face, stung her eyes. But at least the tears that had threatened now seemed as close as the distant road at the end of the lane.

She wondered if she would always feel this confused, this alone.

What if she *were* to marry Reb, as everyone expected? Marriage to him would be no hardship—he was a loving man, true and good down to his toes. Familiar. *Comforting.* And neither of those were qualities to discount. But it was not how it would have been with Griff. She must have subconsciously been trying to figure that out when she'd gone off to Central America to think about whether to marry Reb—even while she must have subconsciously been mourning the loss of that chance with Griff.

Oh, if only she'd said something then! If only he had.

But how would that have changed things?

For even though Reb was having second thoughts about their engagement, some gut instinct told Julia that he *did* love her still— had always loved her—and if she had chosen Griff years and years ago, it would have rent their friendship in two.

Yet how could she stand losing Griff's friendship? That was what had propelled her out here today. She'd realized her fear was not unfounded—and might become reality no matter what she did.

Because at the same moment she'd realized that although Reb's profession was one where the dangers of him being severely injured were inherent, she had chosen marriage with him because it hadn't seemed as risky as one with Griff. And for that lapse in courage, she had no one to blame but herself.

She stumbled, the tears coming at last and nearly blinding her. How could she bear losing him? How?

"Jules! Julia, wait."

She turned to see Griff coming toward her, and she wiped away the tears on her cheeks even as new ones formed in her eyes. No, she would never be able to watch him walk with that catch in his gait and not feel his pain with every step. Would never again be able to look at him and not feel the depth of her love for him, no matter what course their lives took.

Momentarily turning away from him, she hastily dabbed at her eyes with a tissue she found in her jacket pocket.

She turned back to him as he stopped beside her. "Well! So were you sent to console me as the dearest friend Reb and I have?" she asked. "If they only knew what kind of friends we both are!"

His eyes widened at the bitterness in her voice. It shocked her, too, for it was an echo of his tone that evening on his porch. She didn't want to become that kind of woman any more than Griff wanted to be that kind of man, and she knew in a flash that they were both in very real danger of that happening, unless some resolution to this situation could be found that they *could* live with.

"I came on my own," he said, hands dug deep into the pockets of his jacket. He had forgotten his hat, and the tips of his ears were nearly scarlet already from the cold. If it actually was the cold that made them so. "Let people make what they want to about that. I wasn't gonna let you stand out in the middle of the whole outdoors by yourself cryin' your eyes out."

He handed her a handkerchief. She gave it back to him. "Well, as you can see, I'm not crying," she said.

He cracked a wry half smile. "You forget how well I know you. But suit yourself."

Pivoting, he narrowed his eyes in the distance. "Here, let's get out of this wind some."

He took her elbow as he guided her to the shelter of one of the tall pecan trees that lined the lane to the Farley home.

There, he hunched his back as he protected her from the wind. "I thought we'd better get the game plan down before Reb got here tomorrow."

"You mean, get our stories straight." She stared at her boots.

He gave a heavy sigh. "You're not gonna make me feel like I've done somethin' wrong, Julia."

"Really?" She lifted her head and fairly glared at him. "What about that speech just now at the dinner table? What was that?"

"Believe it or not, I was trying to do the right thing." His mouth tightened. "No—I take that back. I was trying to do what you'd like me to. Whatever happens with…you know, someone's bound to end up with some hard feelings, and I thought providin' some perspective on how it not being anyone's fault when people change might help—help everyone to understand when the moment of truth came."

"Oh," Julia said in a small voice. "Then… thank you, I guess."

Griff also scowled at his boot tops for a moment, then said, "I guess I better be honest. I also said that in the dining room so's to leave the door open—should you and I… *you* know."

"Is that so?" A red-tailed hawk circled above, making use of the wind currents so as to concentrate on sighting prey on the ground. Julia watched it, wishing she were as able to adapt. "You heard everyone in there, Griff. It'll cause so many hurt and uncomfortable feelings if Reb and I break it off, and even more should you and I become involved."

"If?" He stared at her, hard. "You can't mean that you're actually thinkin' of going through with the wedding! How could that be right for anyone?"

The hawk swerved away, apparently finding nothing of interest.

"I don't know," Julia said numbly, still watching the hawk. "All I know is that I love him, too, and I promised to marry him. It wouldn't be fair to anyone to say anything until I've settled how I really feel about him in my heart. And I don't think it *will* be settled for some time."

"But—" Griff started to protest, then stopped himself. Out of the corner of her eye she saw him struggling, as she was struggling, to do what was right for everyone, as had always been his particular calling.

Finally he nodded. "Fine, then. I'll leave it up to you to decide whether to say anything to Reb about us and how we feel about each other. And if you want me to step back as you take a crack at figuring out what's going on between you, I'll do it."

"Y-you'd do that?" She looked at him wonderingly. She'd gotten such a different vibe from him at the dinner table. As if he'd rather be dead than see her with another man, even his best friend.

Especially his best friend.

"I would," he said as staunchly as if he were taking an oath. "I've sure learned that steppin' in, declarin' myself, isn't the best way to go about things," he added, not meeting her eyes.

She understood why when he went on. "But if you do decide that the two of you are meant to be, don't ask me to stand there next to Reb and in front of God and the whole town while he makes you his wife." His Adam's apple bobbed as he swallowed hard. "I won't stop it, if that's what you think will make you happy, but I won't be there to watch it."

"I—I guess that would be a lot to expect," Julia said, relieved to have that particular pressure taken off of them both. Yet the band around her heart only tightened instead of easing at his words.

And why would it ease? He looked haggard, as if he'd aged twenty years in the few days since their friendship had changed. The tiny lines fanning from the corners of his eyes that had made him look so rugged now made him look stressed out. Two grooves ran from either side of his nose to his mouth, and gave him the appearance of a man on edge. A bitter edge.

Her heart fuller than it had ever felt, she set a comforting hand on his arm, needing to touch him as a friend.

"I don't know what will happen, Griff. With Reb and me, or you and me. I just don't know. But I do promise I'll do my utmost to do what is right—for me."

"Fair enough." He didn't respond to her

touch, but neither did he pull away. "I guess you should know, though. If you do marry Reb...I think it'd be best if I moved north again."

Julia blinked. Her hand fell from his arm. "Move?"

"Mom's doin' fine." He shifted on his feet. "I'm glad I came back after Dad died, but now—hell, her social life is more active than mine."

"You mean, you'd leave?" At the thought of not having her best friend in her life, her mind harkened back to the time he hadn't been in her life on a daily basis, and it struck her anew how much she had missed him. Missed him as she would have missed a vital limb.

"I'd have to, Julia." He looked like misery itself. "Don't you see? How could I stay now that we know that we love—"

"No!" She pressed her fingers to his mouth. "Please, don't say it. Maybe if we don't say it, it won't affect us. I mean, we did that for years, didn't we? And it worked fine! We were the best of friends!"

He clasped her wrist to move her hand away. "Julia, you can't be serious."

"I'm completely serious—if it means you won't leave."

His eyes turned remote as that cold, hard impassivity took hold of him. It was if she were looking at a complete stranger. It told her that the break had already, irrevocably occurred. "It won't work. If you marry Reb, the only chance you've got—the only chance I've got—is if we cut ties completely."

He grasped her upper arms with a clamp-like grip that made her think he almost wanted to shake her. "Don't you see, Julia? I've stood by, kept my peace, for ten years! Ten years of wondering if I'd ever get over you. At least then I could tell myself that any chance of having your love was hopeless, since it was obvious that you loved Reb. But now that I know...God help me, I'd come to despise myself if I stayed here, living every day with the evidence of my inability to speak up when I had a chance with you."

His gaze dropped. "I have to be honest," he whispered. "I'd come to look down on you, too, Jules—for the same lapse in courage."

He was right. She had not had the courage to let herself love him after almost losing him, and she couldn't do it now, either.

Tears welled in her eyes. "Of course I can't expect you to stay, Griff. Not when you feel that way. But through all this, the one thing

I've concentrated on, the one thing that's kept me going, is that I wouldn't lose your friendship. And now it seems it will happen anyway!"

She buried her face in her hands, no longer able to hold back the sobs.

The wind whistled around them, the sound like air being sucked through a tunnel. It made her bones ache. It made her heart ache—even more than it did already—with its desolateness.

Then Griff whispered raggedly, "Jules. Julia, look at me."

When she couldn't comply, he gripped her wrists, tugging her hands away from her face. She tried to pull away, shaking her head. "No, Griff! Please, I c-can't stand to. It's like we're already strangers, like we're growing more and more distant from each other every minute."

"Look at me."

He lifted her chin and she was forced to meet his gaze. And, oh! in his eyes, those violet-blue eyes she knew as well as her own, she saw the Griff she'd always known.

"Lose me as a friend?" he whispered roughly. "That could never, ever happen in a million years."

He grasped her hand and pressed it to his chest. "Miles won't matter. You'll always be here. Always, no matter what happens."

"Oh, Griff!" She threw herself into his arms, and it was like coming home. "You'll always be in my heart, too. Always," she promised.

His arms tightened around her, and the relief she felt nearly took her breath away. There was still much to be figured out, but she could do it knowing she would not lose his friendship.

She raised her head and could tell that he, too, was relieved that that much was certain. Then, as if her gaze had a will of its own, it drifted slowly downward to his mouth—that wild, tender mouth that had kissed her so passionately… Had it been only a few days ago?

Just the thought of what that kiss had done to her sent desire flaring dangerously deep within her. She must snuff it out somehow—snuff it completely.

No, they both must, for her eyes lifted and it was clear in Griff's gaze that those emotions would always be there between them, whether they acted upon them or not.

She pulled away, and he let her go with the trailing of his fingers down her arm to her wrist to her fingertips, where they both dragged out that most tenuous of touches.

It was an agony to lose that connection with him.

Then suddenly it was there again as he took her hand and pulled her against him. Their mouths met unerringly, melded in a surge of pure, unadulterated longing that had them both foregoing breath to maintain the connection between them.

His hands moved frantically over her body, as if to brand her every curve—as if to memorize them. And she was the same, tearing at the buttons of his jacket so that she could burrow her hands inside, closer to the heat of him that made her warmer than a thousand bonfires.

Oh, to never feel this passion with him again! To never have his lips branding her, to never know how their bodies would fit together in perfect complement, like hand to glove, like two puzzle pieces that only together made a whole.

Then, just as quickly, they stood apart, the yearning a deep crevasse between.

"What will we do, Griff?" Julia whispered, trying to catch her breath. "What will we do?"

"I don't know." His voice was hoarse. "I don't know."

"Hey!" the shout came from a distance.

Their chins both snapped upward.

"Hey, Julia, is that you?"

Julia stepped from her place partially hidden by the pecan trunk. At the end of the lane stood a tall, lanky figure with a duffel bag slung over one shoulder. His legs were as bowed as the wishbone on a chicken. The buckle at his waist was as large as a saucer, and even though the sky was overcast, it shone so bright as gold it may as well have been as sunny out as the Fourth of July.

"R-Reb?" Julia stammered, narrowing her eyes against the sting of the wind rushing past her. Beside her, still hidden by the tree, Griff took an imperceptible step further into its shadow.

"It's me, all right!" Reb started toward her at a clipped gait, then seemed unable to control himself and, dropping the duffel, began to run.

He could have been an Olympic sprinter, for he reached her in seconds and swept her up in a rib-cracking embrace, giving her a resounding kiss that held nothing back and conveyed no sense at all of any hesitation or second thoughts on his part.

And, oh, it was good to feel glad to see him! Julia thought, closing her eyes, her cheek against the soft suede of his jacket front. She had missed Reb and that special element he brought to her life, to the friendship the three of them had together. Her nature was unremittingly earnest. Griff was nothing if not self-contained and introspective. But Reb was out there—everything he felt or thought he wore right there on his sleeve. His wants, his needs, his desires, all of it. He was the buoyancy that kept Griff afloat, while still being the anchor that kept her from taking off after every quest that seemed to present itself.

And strangely, she realized she loved him then as she'd always loved him—would always love him. That hadn't changed and wouldn't change. She didn't know how that could be so. She only knew that it was.

Just as she always had and always would love Griff as she did now.

Reb set her down and beamed at her. She must have been staring at him as if he were a ghost conjured up from out of nowhere, for he laughed, throwing back his head with complete abandon.

"Gotcha, didn't I?" he crowed in that way that was pure Reb—no-holds-barred enthusiasm and emotion. It was so different from the restrained demeanor that she was so used to with Griff, it took Julia aback.

"What are you doing here?" she asked. "Your mother said you were spending Christmas with your agent and his family."

"That'd be the day! George is about as much a family man as stray dog. But I'd say the question is, what are *you* doin' out here, darlin'?" he asked, tipping his hat back on his head so that he looked like no one so much as a young Will Rogers, straight, dark forelock dangling over his forehead, dimples and all. "You couldn't've known I was comin'."

She batted her eyes nervously, wondering if they were still red from her tears. "I just… I wanted…"

Griff stepped out from behind the pecan. "Julia'd needed a little break from the whole family hoo-ha—you know how yours and mine and hers can get when in a bunch—and I came out to keep her company. But now that you're here, I reckon I'm relieved of that duty."

He stuck out his hand. "Welcome home, Reb. It's good to have you back."

Reb peered at his friend in doubt, and for one prolonged moment—it felt like a century—Julia wondered if he suspected what had just taken place between her and Griff.

Then Reb spread his arms, ignoring Griff's outstretched hand, and gave his friend as enthusiastic a hug as he'd given Julia—minus the kiss.

"Damn, but it's good to be back," Reb said, slapping Griff's back as he let him go. "I know it's only been a few months, but it feels like an eon, so much has happened, y'know? George sealed the deal with Justin late last night and the both of us caught red-eyes, him to Puerto Vallarta to bake in the sun and me to Houston by way of Atlanta, if you can believe it. But that was the only connection I could get at this late date."

He aimed his thumb over his shoulder. "Then it took a half hour of convincin'—and a fifty-dollar tip—to get that airport taxi driver to drive all the way out to Bridgewater to drop me off."

He apparently realized he'd been rambling on for several moments without so much as a peep from his two best friends that he asked, "You sure you didn't know I was comin'? I told Mom that made-up story 'bout me spendin' Christmas in L.A., knowing she'd tell you, just so's I could enjoy this moment."

He peered into her face. "I know you said you came out here needing a break, but Mom must've suspected something, otherwise why would y'all be here right in the middle of what's got to be dinnertime?"

"I…we…that is, we didn't know, honest, we didn't," Julia equivocated, panic-stricken that Reb might guess what she and Griff had actually been up to.

"No?" He must have sensed something had changed in his absence, though, for his interested gaze went back and forth from her to Griff, and she wondered if he would bring up the matter of rethinking their wedding, and they could settle it then and there.

But it wasn't something that could be taken care of with a short conversation and a meeting of the minds. Not this. It involved so many people, so many loyalties and loves and wants and needs and desires.

In any case, any moment of truth that might be on the horizon was yet to come, for Reb shrugged that nonchalant cowboy shrug of his and laughed again.

"Well, then," he said. "Looks like I've got

to get a ride back into town and find a place to buy me a lottery ticket."

He grinned at them in outright pleasure. "'cause winnin' the world championship and then coming home to be accidentally met by my two best friends in the whole world? That's got to make me the luckiest man alive!"

REB FETCHED HIS bag and the three of them walked back to the house together, where he was greeted like the prodigal son. Hugging her son, Sue Farley cried from sheer surprise, and he got so many slaps on the back from the rest of the group that Griff wondered if they'd dislodge one of Reb's lungs.

Griff tried with all his might to ignore the possessive arm that his friend kept around Julia even after a place had been set for him center stage and his plate had been piled high with turkey and fixings. Tried to ignore the smoldering indignation that threatened to turn into out-and-out anger that Reb apparently had no qualms about acting as if he'd never sent her that durned letter!

Watching the whole scene balanced on the back two legs of his chair at the end of the table with deceptive equanimity, Griff felt as always like the most inconvenient of fifth wheels. It set the funk he'd sunk into like concrete.

All right, so he could understand that letter wouldn't exactly be the first topic of conversation between the two of them, but how could Reb act as though nothing was wrong? Yet maybe, in his view, there *was* nothing wrong—whatever he'd conveyed in his letter perhaps was not as drastic as Julia may have interpreted. Griff himself hadn't read it. Maybe Reb had said something in the letter that Julia had taken in the wrong vein, when in Reb's mind everything was just peachy keen between them.

Still, Reb *knew* it had concerned Julia! Yet none of that was evident now as he dropped a kiss on her forehead and told her how good it was to see her again, and that she looked just about good enough to eat with a spoon, as their families indulgently clucked and cooed.

Griff's own stomach ground ominously. What if everything that had happened between Julia and himself had been a result of her believing Reb meant to break things off with her in his letter? After all, she had told him not twenty minutes ago that she still loved Reb—and didn't know her own heart enough to say for sure she wouldn't marry him.

Griff desperately tried to believe that he saw puzzlement in Julia's eyes, too, as she looked up at their friend while he went on and on to a captive audience at the dinner table about the deal he'd cut with the boot maker, for that evidently was the true part of the story Reb had told his mother.

"Unfortunately, after the first of the year it's gonna be busier than ever, ramping up for the next rodeo season." Reb was going on about his own matters with what Griff viewed as utter inconsiderateness to what Julia might be feeling right now. "I've got Kyle Fordyce out of Tulsa fast on my heels."

He threw a grin at Griff. "If it weren't for drawing that brute of a bull in his last go-round, he might be sportin' this gold buckle right now rather than me."

"Some people for sure got all the luck," Griff said with just enough bite to elicit a puzzled look from a few of their parents and a quelling one from Julia.

"None of that, Reb," she said loyally. "You won that championship fair and square."

The grateful look that Reb gave her for her

comment made Griff's stomach give another nauseating twist.

"I bet you're just as glad, though, that it's another cowboy and not me who's nursing a couple of busted ribs and a concussion that'll keep him out of the first couple months of the new season," he said.

Julia didn't answer, but her face went white, and Griff knew from the way she avoided Reb's eyes that she was thinking not of her fiancé but of him—Griff—and the injury he'd suffered instead of Reb those years ago.

It was a small bit of satisfaction, but he'd take it.

His gaze shifted from Julia to Reb—who was watching him with interest.

"Say, Griff," he said after ducking his head to tuck a forkful of dressing into his cheek, "now that I'm in a groove and got some funds to spare, I've been thinkin'—why don't you come on board as my manager? I could use someone with good cow sense watchin' my backside."

Griff's chair came forward onto all four legs with a *thunk*. "You want me…to go on the road with you?" he asked Reb.

"Can't think of anyone else who could

do the job better. I'd pay you top wages, of course."

There was a moment of total silence at the table, and then everyone started talking at once.

"What a great idea!" Gary exclaimed. "Your mama and me would feel so much better 'bout you competin' so hard knowing Griff was along making sure you weren't takin' any unnecessary risks."

Frannie's concerned gaze darted to her son. "Griff's got a job, working for Connor."

Connor shrugged. "I'd hate to lose the best manager a ranch could have, but I'd never keep you from grabbin' hold of whatever opportunities came your way, Griff."

What in hell was going on here? Griff wondered. It wasn't that he thought Reb's offer was a token one. It was simply so…so out of the blue.

"But…you've got a manager, Reb," was all Griff could manage to say.

"Yeah, but he's not *you*, y'know?" Reb said. He extended an open hand across the table toward his friend. "Come on, Griff. It'd be like old times. Or almost. I mean, Julia here isn't into following me around the circuit—not that I expect her to—but it gets pretty lonely out there on the road."

Griff's gaze went automatically to Julia's as he recalled their conversation not an hour ago about him doing just as Reb was suggesting: leaving Bridgewater—and her. He remembered her frenzied reaction to his musings, too…a reaction he'd never witnessed in her at Reb's departure.

She only looked at him with the same longing that wore away at him like the steady erosion of the wind across the range.

Then his gaze shifted back to Reb, who settled both arms around Julia's waist with linked hands. Griff had never seen such a silent declaration of ownership.

"And if I can't have my best girl travelin' with me," Reb went on, looking around the table at the gathering, "I can think of nothing I'd like better than to have my best friend in the world at my side."

Chapter Eight

Griff gazed across the herd of Hereford, expertly appraising each white face, looking for the signs of discontent or sluggishness that could mean anything from scours to sore udders. He'd lost less than ten cows this season, a personal best for him. It was a fine record, one he didn't intend to see go down the toilet this far into the year.

It was four days till the new year started the clock rolling again. Three until Reb's championship celebration. Griff had made a career out of avoiding his friend—and Julia—since Christmas Day, first because he needed some time to sort through what Reb's offer meant.

Turning his cow pony, Pete, back toward the ranch, Griff mulled the matter over in his mind for what had to be the hundredth time. He knew Reb well enough to know that the offer had been sincere, but why now? Why not five or six years ago when he'd started his run for the gold buckle? It had more to do with having more money available now. There had to be some reason that Reb wanted Griff by his side now.

If he accepted Reb's offer, it would certainly get him out of Bridgewater and put the distance he knew he needed between himself and Julia. But it would put him in close contact with Reb—the closest Griff would ever have been with his friend—and to be so with the man she belonged to…well, he'd as soon jump in front of a bull again as put himself through that.

And that brought up the second reason he'd avoided his two best friends, which was that he didn't trust himself not to say something, do something, even *feel* something that might give away how he felt about Julia—and she about him. She'd asked him to let her take care of her relationship with Reb, and Griff meant to let her do that without his interference.

Except that was going to be durned difficult, because who should he see riding toward him across the range right now but Reb Farley.

Typically, he came at an all-out gallop,

looking like the Lone Ranger himself on a palomino Griff recognized from the Tanglewood string.

Griff could only ride at a gallop in short bursts, and then only when he really needed to. The exertion of gripping the horse's sides between his knees tended to over-fatigue his injured thigh, giving him less control, so that one unexpected turn or twist could result in him going down.

And he'd been there, done that enough to know he didn't want to go there again if he could help it.

Reb came to a quick stop in front of him, a grin of delight on his face. "Hoo-ey, it feels good to climb aboard an animal for once and know it ain't on a mission from hell not only to buck you off but to see if it can put you in the hospital good and proper."

Griff winced involuntarily.

Reb saw the grimace and was immediately contrite. "Dang, I'm sorry, Griff! I've been out on the circuit where every cowboy jokes about that kind of killer bust-up happenin' to keep himself from freezing in his boots with fear that it will."

He reached across the space between them and gave his friend a slap on the back. "I guess I forget that that exact thing happened to you 'cause you never talk about it."

Griff squinted into the distance. It was exactly what Julia had accused him of.

When he didn't answer, Reb cleared his throat and went on. "Well, it sure don't seem to hold you back a bit. Why, Connor was tellin' me just now when I came out to the ranch to find y'all that Tanglewood is lucky as hell to have a ranch manager like you." Reb shot Griff a sidelong glance. "Kinda made me wonder if he'd changed his mind 'bout not holding you back, should ya want to come on as my manager."

"I think you can take Connor Brody at his word," Griff supplied. He lifted his reins and clicked his tongue. Pete started to walk for the gate, and Reb's mount fell in beside them.

"So have you thought 'bout the offer?" Reb asked flat-out, Reb-like. "I know you like to ponder on things for a while, so I've been tryin' to give you some breathin' room to think about it."

That struck Griff as ironic. "And I know you like to settle things quick. At least most of the time."

He focused on a spot between Pete's black

ears, mentally chiding himself for the slip, but his friend must have caught his drift.

"No doubt you're referrin' to how long it's taken for me and Jules to set a weddin' date," Reb said.

Now Griff stared at him. "So...have you?" he made himself ask.

"Nah, it's still up for grabs." He peered at his friend across the gap between them. "But I expect somethin' will be decided soon. I just wanted to wait to make sure I had the championship in hand before we got into wedding plans...wanted to wait till I had something to offer Julia."

"But what about your letter?" Griff blurted in total mystification.

"Yeah, my letter." Reb gave a gusty sigh. "I must've been having one helluva panic attack when I wrote that."

Griff's heart sank. So Reb *had* been having a rash of second thoughts, and that was all. He still intended to marry Julia, from the sounds of it. But would she still have him for her husband?

At the thought, the words were out of his mouth before he could stop them. "So are you over your panic attack or doubts or whatever it was? Do you mean to be the kind of husband to her she deserves?" Griff demanded.

The friendly expression on Reb's face never changed, but there was no doubt that a certain steeliness had entered his gaze. "I believe that conversation is one between Julia and myself."

"Then when did you plan on having that particular talk with her? Because I want to know what your intentions are!"

"My *intentions?*" Reb repeated, raising his eyebrows.

This was not going well, Griff thought. He recalled how at the very beginning, when Julia had thrown herself into his arms at the tack and feed, that he had sworn to himself that he would conduct himself with the utmost of honor and integrity. It had been his only hope at that point, he'd figured, of winning her.

Well, along the way he'd slipped up—royally so, and more than once—and it had cost him, hadn't it? Still, even if he didn't have a stake in the matter any longer, he couldn't keep his mouth shut and let things slide. Not when Julia's happiness was the real stake.

They'd reached the gate, and Griff dismounted to unlatch it. But his gloved hand paused on the catch, and he swung around angrily to face his friend.

"Durn it, Reb, you dropped that letter on her like a bomb three weeks ago, and any fool can see that this limbo you've put her in is hurting her. There's no way I'll let her walk into that big homecoming celebration in a few days without the situation resolved."

Reb also dismounted. "Since you're not Julia's father or brother, maybe what *I'd* like to know is what right you have to take such an attitude with me?"

Griff tore his gloves off and tossed them on the ground before squaring off in front of Reb. "So she's not my sister or whatever, she's my friend, that's what right I have!"

"But she's *my* fiancée." Reb's own gloves came off, landing next to Griff's on the grass. "So you tell me how that makes anything between Julia and me your business—*friend.*"

His implication was clear. Griff could feel his face turn red with suppressed anger. And guilt. Still, he wasn't about to back down. Not now.

Griff stepped nose to nose with him. "Come on, Reb! Julia's been like a bird on a live wire since you wrote. Believe me, you fail to come completely clean with her on what's goin' on inside you, you'll answer to me! And you aren't so high and mighty I can't whip your ass if I want to, just like I did a score of times when we were growin' up!"

Reb's chin jutted. "You mean, like I whipped *yours* regularly."

"In your dreams." Griff raised his arm, but it was only to wave four fingers in his friend's face. "I can keep track on one hand the number of fights against me you won!"

"That's only because you obviously can't count!" Reb shouted back.

Hat brim to hat brim, stances wide, jaws bulging, they stared at each other for one long, indeterminable moment.

Then Reb said quietly, "We never fought about Julia, though, did we?"

Griff blinked. They'd sure about everything else. Who was going to take the NFL division title, the Cowboys or the Oilers. Who was going to test drive the old Ford pickup the two boys had bought together on their sixteenth birthday. Who'd pick up the tab for beers after Reb won his first big rodeo purse.

And who was going to take Web Corbin's prize fishing tackle after he died. Griff had wanted Reb to have it. Reb had refused, saying his friend would want it someday to pass on to his own son.

That was when it hit Griff. Strangely, it felt as if he'd been picked up and dropped back in that corral ten years ago.

For, once again, he was placed in that most impossible of situations: at odds with his best friend.

The bristle in his spine dissolved all of a sudden, and he slumped against the fence post. Yes, Reb was his friend. His *best friend,* the brother he never had, the one guy who knew him best. And whom he knew best.

It was a bond, as strong as the one between Julia and himself, and one that she could never share in.

"No, we never fought about Julia," he said, shaking his head slowly. "Maybe we should have."

"Maybe." Reb slouched against the railing next to him, and the two men stood side by side, fists now crammed into the pockets of their jackets, chins down as they studied their boot tops for a long moment.

Finally, Reb sighed. "You want me to be straight, Griff, I'll be straight. I could tell way back in junior high that you and Julia had feelings for each other."

"I guess I knew you knew," Griff admitted.

"But I didn't know how deep those feelings went, and at a certain point I figured, what the hey, I might as well throw my hat into the ring."

Griff hunched his shoulders against the wind whistling past his ears. "Yeah, but you did it when I was laid up with a gash five inches long in my leg from takin' on a bull *you* riled up."

He was glad to have that matter out in the open at last. And surprisingly, there was no rancor in his voice—none of the bitterness that he'd been sorely afraid he'd hear there for the rest of his life.

"You think I don't know that?" Reb asked. "That my best friend took the hit for me? I knew you'd done that 'cause you loved me like the brother neither of us ever had."

"And I'd do it again, Reb," he told his friend gruffly. "In a heartbeat."

Reb nodded. "I know—just like I've known for a couple of years now that you still love Julia, more than you ever have."

Griff shot upright, too shocked to dissemble. "How could you know that? I never told a soul, not one soul!"

"Yeah, but you left your family and hometown, everything you cared most about! Why would a man do that 'Cept to try to forget and move on?"

Reb pushed off from the railing and stooped to snatch a few blades of grass from the ground, only to immediately fling them away from him to scatter like confetti. "I just haven't known for sure how Julia really, truly felt—not so much about you, but about me."

He looked at Griff searchingly. "I guess I wrote her that letter tryin' to find out," he said.

Griff knew it had been hard for him to admit such a thing—that Reb's doubts had not been about his own love but Julia's love for him.

He dropped his chin, avoiding his friend's gaze under cover of lifting his hat to run his hand through his hair. "I haven't exactly had a direct line to her thoughts on the matter."

No, he had to be honest, or as honest as he could be at a moment like this. "I know she was devastated when she got your letter. And I know that one of her biggest fears is that—" He swallowed and made himself go on. "That when all's said and done, she might lose your friendship."

"That could never happen," Reb said fervently. "Never."

"That's what I told her."

Hand on his hips and chin down, Reb toed back into place a divot of turf that had been dug up by the stray hoof of a horse or cow.

"So what you're sayin' is I need to have that conversation with Julia." He cracked a wry half smile. "How'd you put it? 'Come completely clean with her with what's goin' on inside me'? Good grief, who on God's green earth ever does that, even with themselves?"

Griff shrugged, not wanting to speak, not wanting to hope that, should Reb and Julia talk honestly, that she would say what *she* needed to say. To do so meant wishing for the unhappiness of one of his friends, and he couldn't do that, no matter what. He could only do what he'd done from the beginning and stay out of it—remain silent as he'd kept his peace for almost ten years.

Still, *he* had one more thing to say.

"I'd like to thank you for your offer to be your manager, but I'm turnin' it down," Griff said. "It was kind of you, Reb, but... I need to do what's right for me, and that's goin' north again, maybe Colorado this time."

He hesitated, then made himself go on.

"And just so's you know," he said, his voice hoarse, "no matter what happens, you won't lose my friendship, either."

Reb peered at him curiously for a long moment. Then he turned his head to focus intently on some sight in the distance, although Griff couldn't have said what. He saw Reb's Adam's apple bob in his throat.

"You're a good friend, Griff," he finally said.

Griff nodded again, this time because he couldn't have spoken, even if he'd wanted to.

But then, that seemed the role he was destined to fulfill in this life.

JULIA SET THE phone receiver back it its cradle and made another check on her list. So the decorations were made and ready to go up New Year's Eve afternoon. A cake in the shape of Texas and blazoned with the Lone Star flag was being decorated by Frannie Corbin and would be ready to pick up about the same time. Since this was a family affair, there were to be games for children twelve and under in the Sunday School room, and a special area in the church hall for the teenagers.

The band was signed, the kegs already

chilling. All the event lacked was the guest of honor, and he was primed and ready to go, as well.

Julia's pen stilled on the paper as she became lost in thought. Had it only been a few days ago that Reb had come back to Bridgewater? It seemed so much longer—an agony of time in which the two of them talked of everything and anything except their relationship. And for that, she had to take at least half the blame. She hadn't had the courage to bring the subject up, especially with Reb acting as if he had never sent that letter to her, never raised any doubts between them.

That he would behave so made her heart incredibly heavy, because it told her that he did know something was wrong.

She glanced around at the knock at the front door. The knob turned, and Reb himself peeked inside.

"Well, my luck is for sure holdin'. I'd hoped to find you home this afternoon," he said cheerfully.

"I'm just clearing up the last details for the party, is all," she said, rising to go greet him. She was surprised when, instead of his usual hug and peck on the cheek, he stood with his hat firmly grasped in both hands, and gave her a nod.

"Well, far be it from me to keep y'all from puttin' on the dog on account of me," he joked. "But if you can spare a few minutes to talk, I'd sure appreciate it."

Julia detected the purpose behind his banter. She felt suddenly calm that the moment of truth, as it were, was at hand. Nothing could be worse than this agony of not knowing where they stood—or where they were going.

"Let's have a seat in the living room," she offered.

There, Julia glanced around at the familiar surroundings—the glass case displaying her mother's collection of leaded crystal that was to be Julia's after her marriage, the shelves lined with well-loved books and old family photos of her brother and her as children, tow-headed and sunburned. Of them not much older with their father, sitting upon the very same swing that was outside on the porch. Of her father and mother on their wedding day, looking about as in love as two people could. Of the "whole shootin' match," as Web Corbin used to call it when their family, the Farleys and the Sennetts all got together.

Abruptly, she remembered how her father

had sounded, talking about Frannie Corbin and how it was an impossibility for him to share the rest of his life with her, after he'd called her husband friend. What she realized now was that, if anything, Andy Sennett had made a career of not speaking of his special regard for Frannie and would continue forever to do so. For to speak meant risking the best thing in his life, and it was better to have his friendship with Griff's mother than not at all.

Julia turned away from the photo, for some reason unable to look at it any longer, to find Reb gazing at her with an expression she'd never seen in his eyes.

"What is it, Reb?" she asked gently, setting her hand on his knee.

He grasped it in his and held on. "I took a ride out to Tanglewood to see Griff this afternoon," he said. "He's been so scarce, I was afraid I'd go away again having barely two minutes with my best friend."

"Managing the ranch keeps him pretty busy," Julia murmured noncommittally.

He gave a short laugh. "Not so busy that he didn't have a minute to dress me down proper for that letter of mine."

"Really?" Her heart gave a mighty thump, one she realized came from fearing not that

Griff had confronted Reb with his feelings, but, crazily, that he had not. "W-what did he say?"

"That you'd been worried sick about what I meant, and that I needed to talk to you about it." He sent her a lopsided grin. "About how you both decided my letter was more about me havin' a doozy of a case of the weddin' bell jitters and less about callin' off the engagement for real, givin' me the benefit of the doubt."

Her heart settled back into its rhythm. "Oh. I see."

"But…but my cold feet wasn't all the letter was about," he admitted slowly, the smile slipping away from his face as he gazed at her earnestly. "There was more to it. More…more doubts. *My* doubts."

She could see how hard this conversation was for him, so she shifted on the sofa and tucked her leg beneath her to face Reb more fully.

"Then tell me what they were," she urged. "What are your hesitations now? You owe it to me to be honest. Griff's right. I need to know what you want to do about our engagement."

Chin down, he fiddled with the diamond

engagement ring on her hand. "I guess that depends on what *you* want to do about our engagement."

"I will say that I never had any doubts about us before you wrote me that letter," Julia began, then bit her lip. Heaven knew she wanted to be honest with him, to be the kind of forthright and genuine person she'd always prided herself as being. Yet how could she hurt the best friend she'd ever had by telling him she'd discovered she also loved the best friend he'd ever had?

"Now, though," she whispered, "I don't know."

"But you have had doubts about me in the past," Reb said. "I know you did—that was why you went to Central America."

Julia nodded slowly. "Yes, I went there to work them through. But once I said I'd marry you, Reb, I never looked back," she assured him.

"Still, you went away to work through your doubts." His gaze locked with hers, the hurt she wanted to spare him from, there, regardless. "You didn't work them through with me."

"Well, now I want to work through our doubts—yours and mine—with you. I truly do."

His gaze searched hers for a long moment. Then he rose and paced away from her to the window, where he stared out at the street, hands jammed into his back pockets.

"You can't stand to watch me ride the bulls," he finally said, still facing away from her. "It's what I do for a living. It's what I love. And you can't watch me do it, Jules."

"I'm sorry for that, Reb." She sat with her fingers tensely knitted together in her lap. "I just… I'm just so afraid of what might happen to you."

"The thing is, I think the reason you can't stand to watch me ride the bulls is not 'cause you're afraid of what might happen to me."

"What do you mean? I couldn't stand to see you get hurt, Reb!" What was he thinking—that she didn't care?

Then he looked at her over his shoulder, and his face was infinitely sad. "Sure, but the reason you can't watch me ride is 'cause of what you saw happen to Griff."

Her heart took up its bass drum thumping again. "You're right. It was a horrible thing to witness, and I don't want ever to see you go through that—"

"But it's Griff you see, not me," Reb persisted, turning to face her.

She stood, barely registering that she did so. "Because he got hurt in front of my eyes—"

"No, it's because it's always been Griff. You've always loved Griff, Julia."

She stared at him. He looked back at her with steadiness she'd hardly ever seen in him. It was more Griff's way.

"You…you know?" she asked in a quiet voice.

"Yes."

Her cheeks were wet, she realized, touching them with her fingertips. "Am I the only one among the three of us who *didn't* know my heart?" she said.

Reb shook his head. "No, darlin'. I think I've always known, too, but didn't want to deal with it, either."

His mouth twisted. "Well, I'm sure as hell havin' to deal with it now. So are you—and so is Griff."

They stood apart, separated by the width of the room—and, it seemed to Julia, so much more. The late afternoon sun slanted through the window behind him, casting his features into relief. They looked jagged in the sharp winter light, like the face of a limestone cliff.

She ached for him and for herself. She

wanted to go back to before this whole situation began, but just where was that point in time? Before Reb asked her to marry him? Before he, Griff and she became inseparable? Before they'd been born?

"So you see why it wouldn't really be the best choice for us to marry, Julia," Reb finally said. "Not the best choice for you, and not for me. I think we make really good best friends, and many a marriage has not only survived but thrived on that kind of foundation. But it wouldn't be right for us—not when you love someone else."

"I don't know what to say, Reb." She blinked back more tears, just barely succeeding. "Sorry doesn't seem to be enough."

"Hell, what's to be sorry for?" He actually gave her one of his old devil-may-care grins. "It's been an honor havin' you as my girl. I wouldn't change a minute. Not a single minute."

"Me, either," she whispered.

He held out his hand, and she went into his arms to be held close by him, as he'd done innumerable times before. But it was different this time, while still being the same as always: familiar. *Comforting.*

Julia closed her eyes in relief and hugged Reb back with all her might.

"To be perfectly honest, Jules? I'm the only one who should be sorry," he murmured. "I just wanted you so bad I was willin' to do whatever it took to win you. To keep you. But the only thing I want more than you, Jules, is your happiness."

He lifted his head and tenderly smoothed a lock of her hair back from her face, his hand lingering on her cheek. "I ignored every single sign that you and Griff had feelings for each other. And that's not your fault. It's not anyone's fault to fall in love with who you do."

Julia smiled through her tears, which had started up again despite her efforts to hold them at bay. "That's what Griff said."

"Well, he's right, y'know. He's right about a lot of things."

She wondered what he meant by that.

"We should probably talk about how to tell our families," Julia said. "Would you like to wait until after your celebration tomorrow night to tell them the engagement is off?"

"I'll be frank, Jules—if it'd suit you, I'd like to do that." He shook his head ruefully. "Mom gave me an idea of what everyone's got in store for me. I haven't told this to a soul, but I'd give just about anything to get out of goin' tomorrow night and havin' everybody treat me like a conquerin' hero. I'm just a regular cowboy."

"Not to them," she told him. "And not to me, either."

His eyes lit up with that old Reb-look she'd somehow feared she'd never see again—affectionate, caring. "That means a lot to me, Julia. Just as it means a lot to me that we're still friends."

"Yes, friends," Julia answered, barely able to speak around the lump in her throat. It just seemed such a miracle to her that the friendship with Reb she'd so feared would change beyond recognition because of their involvement was not destroyed but still intact, if not stronger.

And she couldn't help thinking, if it could be so with this best friend, dare she hope that she might have the same chance of such a thing happening with Griff?

GRIFF TURNED HIS sheepskin collar up against the nip in the air as he headed up the street to the Sennett home. Winter had set in for good, it seemed. Every bit of vegetation had turned brown due to lack of rain, actually, rather than cold. It made for a dull four months. Winter had been a heck of a lot colder up north, but at least the snow frosting the ground and trees had made a stunning picture that had its up-lifting merits.

He tried to focus on that, how it would be a nice change from south central Texas. But the very thought of moving away again, for the very same reason he had before—made him feel even more cheerless.

He climbed the porch steps and knocked, only then wondering why Julia's father had asked him over this morning.

Andy himself answered the door, a huge smile wreathing his face.

"Griff! Get yourself in out of the cold, son." Andy clapped Griff on the back as he shut the door behind him. "I hope we don't get any precip to go with these low temps. We don't need people driving through freez-ing rain to get to Reb's celebration tomor-row night."

"I hate to be the one to tell you this, Andy, but a little ice won't keep people in these parts from a good old-fashioned New Year's Eve party."

Andy laughed. "Too true!" He gestured down the hallway. "Come on in the den here."

Griff entered the Sennetts' den and stopped cold at the sight of his mother and Julia chatting on the sofa.

Julia looked up at him, eyes wide with surprise, too—and sudden apprehension. That his presence would evoke such a response in her put him in a fouler mood than he already was.

Griff gave her a nod and another to his mother without saying anything, for Andy had bustled into the room behind him and was standing expectantly in front of the fireplace mantel.

Puzzled, Griff took a seat in the easy chair catercorner to Julia.

Andy cleared his throat theatrically. "I guess you kids are wondering why I asked you here today," he said.

Frannie smiled at her son timorously. "It's because we wanted you, our children, to be the first to know."

Griff shook his head. "Know what, Mom?"

She shot Andy a nervous look, and he crossed at once to take her hand. She stood, and they linked their arms around each other's waists as if it were the most natural thing in the world for them to do so.

Andy cleared his throat yet again. "Griff... Julia... It's probably gonna be hard for you to believe this—I know I find it hard to believe every day, but..."

"Believe what, Dad?" Julia asked, obviously as puzzled as Griff.

Andy cast a sidelong glance at Frannie that was ladened with meaning, and his mother smiled back luminously.

That's when Griff caught on: they were in love.

"Mom?" he said, thunderstruck. He glanced at Julia, who seemed to have caught on, as well, for she sat still as stone.

"What we're tryin' to say is—" Frannie began.

"We're getting married!" Andy finished for her.

The ensuing silence was deafening.

"Married?" was all Griff could say.

His mother's delicate eyebrows knit above her eyes. "Now, I know it must be a shock—although not that big of a shock. After all, Andy and I have been seeing a lot of each other in the past year."

"Sure, but...you're getting married?" Griff

asked, knowing he was being obtuse but unable to stop himself. Truthfully, he *had* known Andy Sennett was sweet on his mother, but he'd never thought the older man would voice those sentiments, much less put them into action by asking Frannie to marry him!

"I bet it's a surprise to you, too, darlin'," after I told you not so long ago that it didn't feel right to me to think of my best friend's wife that way," Andy said to his daughter.

"It does have me wondering," Julia admitted without inflection. Griff couldn't tell what feelings she was experiencing at that moment, but her face was uncommonly pale and her eyes glazed, so he'd have to bet she was as confounded as he was.

"It's just that after we had that conversation, I started thinkin'," Andy explained. "Started examining my heart. It wasn't that I didn't think Frannie here could feel that way for me, too. It was wanting with her the same kind of deep and abidin' love that she had in her marriage with Web. What I had with your mother. I didn't believe it possible—thought I'd go the rest of my life pinin' for that kind of love."

His Adam's apple bobbed with the emotion

of his feelings, and Frannie set a supportive hand on his arm.

He must have drawn courage from that contact, for he went on more strongly. "That's when I figured it out—that it couldn't be the same," he said, still addressing Julia, his eyes all for Frannie, tucked against his side. "But it could be something different, even something more."

"Andy's always been a good, good friend to me—to Web, too," Frannie said, her gaze as transfixed. "It's taken some time for me, too, to reconcile that part. I had a good life with Web, and he'll always be in my heart."

Her mouth trembled. "Maybe having that kind of happiness is what made me know that if I was so lucky as to have a chance at that again with Andy, I'd be nine times a fool not to take the risk."

Their parents could have been talking about their children. Griff couldn't even think of glancing at Julia right now, as again the silence rose up and surrounded them.

"We hoped you'd both be happy for us," Frannie finally said, her voice quavering.

Griff didn't answer, dimly registering that Julia rose to her feet, her face even more pale.

"Dad, Frannie, we *are*—very happy," she

said, her voice strained. She made a motion for him to stand, as well. "In fact, we couldn't be more delighted, could we, Griff?"

Griff felt as if he were riveted to the easy chair. He had to admit it—no, he wasn't delighted. All he could think about, in the face of his mother and Andy Sennett taking a chance on love after all they'd been through, both of them losing spouses too early in life... well, his own inaction, his unwillingness to speak all those years seemed more damning than ever.

He had blown his second chance with Julia, and he would never forgive himself for that.

Then Andy said, "You were the one, to tell the truth, who got me started thinkin' that I might have a chance of making my life with Frannie, Griff."

"Me?" he said, blinking.

"Sure. At the dinner table on Christmas. You said that everything was bound to change, the relationships with those we love more than anything. But that change wasn't necessarily bad, and could actually be good, if things needed to change."

His expression became somber, as if he were already saying his wedding vows. "Oh, I still had to come to terms with how it might set with my best friend. Once I asked the question honestly in my heart, it was like he spoke to me. And what he said was that what he wanted—what he'd always and ever would want—is for Frannie to be happy. And if I could do that for her, then I'd have his eternal gratefulness."

"You never told me that!" Frannie cried, staring at Andy in sheer disbelief. Sheer love.

"I'm tellin' you now," he said hoarsely. "I love you, Frannie Corbin."

He took his future bride in his arms as Julia and Griff glanced away from observing the private moment—and at each other at last.

"And we couldn't be more delighted, could we, Griff?" Julia repeated softly.

It was the longing in her voice that snapped him out of his funk but good. It sounded so much like the day when she'd come tearing into the tack and feed and flung herself into his arms, begging him to help her understand Reb's letter and what his doubts might mean. Asking him to be the friend she needed— needed like no one else on earth—to help her figure out what had changed.

Change wasn't necessarily a bad thing in a relationship, not if things need to change.

But Julia had made it pretty durned clear to

him that she didn't want to risk things changing by being in a romantic relationship with him.

Yet now…now, there was something new in her eyes, something different that he'd never seen there before, that made him feel suddenly more hopeful than he had since he was fifteen, leaning on a rail fence as he looked up into the face of the girl he adored—and had known in his heart that she felt the same way.

Somehow things would work out. They had to. Julia and Reb were his best friends, with a bond that went back to the womb, practically. He didn't know how they'd make sense of it all, but they would.

"I am," he said, standing at last. "Delighted, that is. I can't think of two people more made for each other."

"Oh, Griff!" his mother cried.

Tears poured down Julia's and Frannie's cheeks as they hugged. A lump settled crosswise in his own throat as he gave Julia's father a hug, then have his mother one.

"Is this really all right with you, Griff?" she asked.

"Of course it's all right, Mom," he told her

sincerely. "You couldn't ask for a better man than Andy Sennett."

"At least if you want to go on the road with Reb as his manager, you can follow your heart and not have to worry about me being alone. That's why we wanted to tell you now."

She lovingly took his face in her hands. "I'll never forget the sacrifice you made, coming back to live in Bridgewater after your father died. But you must now—you must do what your heart tells you, go where it leads you," she whispered. "All I want is for you to be happy."

It took clearing his throat three times before Griff could speak. "And all I want is for you to be happy, Mom," he said.

Then Andy held out his arm, and Frannie slipped from her son's embrace to his.

"Well, much as we'd like to hang around jaw-jacking, we've got an appointment with a jeweler in Houston to pick out an engagement ring," Andy announced.

"All I want is matching gold bands, I told you," Frannie fretted, although not with much vehemence as Andy helped her on with her jacket.

"We'll see," Julia's father said cryptically, shrugging into his own jacket. "Oh, one more thing—don't worry, Julia, 'bout Frannie and me stealing Reb's thunder tomorrow night. In fact, I think we'd kind of like to keep the news just between the four of us for a while, if you don't mind."

"We don't mind," Julia assured them, her face growing pink, like a girl ten years younger. Griff didn't know what that glow was about, but he chose to take it as a good sign.

"No, we don't mind," he echoed.

Chapter Nine

After their parents left, Griff and Julia stood without speaking for a long moment. The tension, it struck him, was about as thick as it could be without needing a hacksaw to cut it. He'd have sacrificed his Christmas bonus for the next ten years to know what she was thinking right now.

"Well, tomorrow night's gonna be one hell of an interesting time, knowin' our parents are getting married but havin' to keep it a secret," he finally commented, for lack of anything more enlightening to say. What he really wanted to say, one didn't just burst out with like a bronco buster from a chute. He'd already learned that lesson.

"Interesting's an…interesting way to put it," Julia said. She laughed a trifle nervously, avoiding his gaze, which made Griff wonder if his instincts had been right, and she had gotten the same meaning from her father's words as he had—if she'd experienced the same renewal of hope that with love, somehow things would work out for them all.

He didn't dare hope, even contemplate, that she and Reb had broken off with each other. He couldn't wish for that. But Griff would have given his right arm to know if they'd talked—and what the outcome of their conversation had been.

It wouldn't do to push the matter with Julia, however, not when he'd just received another message, clear as a bell, telling him to once again be the friend she needed him to be.

"Rest assured I won't spill the beans about your dad and my mom at Reb's celebration tomorrow night, if you're anxious about that," he said, leaning an arm on the fireplace mantel. "I wouldn't do that to him...or you."

One side of her mouth curled ironically upward. "If anyone gives it away, it'll be the two of them. They couldn't keep their eyes off of each other just now, they're so much in love."

"Well, sure, but they've managed to keep their feelings hidden for a long time—from each other, in fact. So one more day won't hurt."

Somehow he didn't think he was easing Julia's mind, for she suddenly asked, "Won't it?"

"Won't…what?" Griff said, puzzled.

"Won't one more day hurt of keeping feelings secret that you've had for a long, long time?" she answered, pensively tucking a lock of her blond hair behind her ear. "I don't know, but it seems to me it might. I mean, the way he sounded just a week ago, Daddy would rather have died than do something to dishonor his friend's memory or to cause your mother pain. I'd never have thought he'd speak."

Whether she meant them to or not, Griff felt the sting of her words in his heart.

"Do you think he should never have spoken up?" he asked hoarsely.

She shook her head slowly. "No. He obviously did the right thing, especially with the way it turned out. It's just…"

"Or are you thinking the two of them would never have gotten together if things had worked out differently between us?" he asked, trying to help her out.

She looked at him in surprise. "Meaning?"

"Meaning… I don't know." He shrugged, a little frustrated. "Maybe that if we'd gotten involved, you know that neither of our parents would consider marriage to each other, no matter what."

"Does that mean you no longer believe we have a chance?"

Distractedly, he picked a wrought-iron candlestick from off the mantel and set it back down again. Once again, things were not going well. Had he really only imagined the look in her eyes a few moments ago?

If only he knew what she wanted of him! To speak or not to speak. To stay or not to stay. To let himself love her or not.

"Well, not to put too fine a point on it, you're still with Reb," Griff said. "In my book, that kind of hinders a relationship between us even getting started."

"*You* could always speak up." She looked a little frustrated herself, with the way she paced to the sofa but did not take a seat. "Tell him how you feel about me, what you feel you can offer me that he might not be able to. Make a stand."

"Is that what you want?" He peered at her in complete bafflement. "'cause I got the message loud and clear that you wanted to handle that situation. It was between you and Reb."

"And I have handled it." She lifted her chin. "Everything's resolved between Reb and me."

He couldn't ask the question. Didn't want to know the answer—that he was a loser again in the contest between himself and his best friend.

And if so, what was this all about?

"Well, good, I guess," he finally said, cursing himself for his reticence. "If you were able to work things out, then how could I be anything but glad for you?"

"Is that what you want, Griff? That we work things out and I should marry Reb?" she asked, and now there was no question of her frustration. It showed in every stiff line of her body.

Well, he was pretty durned frustrated himself. What did she *want* from him?

What did she need from him?

"You *know* my feelings on the subject, Julia." He pushed off from the mantel, and the move seemed pointedly without direction. "But you're the one who said being together wasn't worth risking our friendship."

The chin lifted a notch higher. "Maybe that's because, for ten years, it wasn't worth the risk to you."

"Well, maybe *that* was because, for ten years, I was under the impression that you'd made the choice to love Reb instead," he retorted. "And don't tell me that wasn't because *you* were afraid to risk loving me!"

They stared at each other as Griff's heart sank to his toes. For he was at that old impasse again—damned if he did, and damned if he didn't. He ought to be taken out back and shot for the fool he was for hoping the situation might have changed. The fact of the matter was, it hadn't. Because the two of them hadn't changed. There was still something within them both that made them afraid to risk and love completely.

Maybe what they were dealing with here had nothing to do with Reb but was actually one of those star-crossed situations right out of a novel, where two people loved each other and yet, because of some fatal flaw each had, weren't meant to be together.

And maybe what was needed was for him to cross the room and take her in his arms to kiss her with all the love he felt for her that couldn't be denied.

How, though, did one know the difference?

He'd be durned if he knew how to foresee such things. Hell, he didn't even have twenty-twenty hindsight, otherwise he wouldn't be standing here aching like he did, watching Julia aching as she did.

"I need to get back out to Tanglewood," he said distractedly, glancing around for his hat and remembering that Andy had taken it at the door. He headed there now. "If we are in for freezing rain, I'll need to gather the herd from the far pastures."

At the doorway, he was stopped by Julia asking, "Will you make it tomorrow night if the weather turns bad?"

Griff paused, head down. There was something in her voice that still got to him, and he supposed always would.

He nodded without turning. "I'll be there," he said. "I wouldn't let down my best friends in the whole world."

"THERE YOU ARE, Miss Sennett!"

Julia turned and peered down the crowded store aisle to see her pupil, Kelly, dodging post-Christmas shoppers in pursuit of her teacher.

The little girl braked in front of Julia just in time. She was out of breath, as if she'd run all the way across town.

Julia stooped to take her shoulders. "Kelly! What are you doing here by yourself? Have you been looking for me?"

"Yes! I need to talk to you." She gulped air. "Right away."

Julia guessed from the look on Kelly's face that it was urgent. Some sixth sense also told her that it was about Jace Larrabie, the boy she had a crush on.

Glancing around for a place where they could have some privacy, Julia spotted the garden section. Chances were they'd be undisturbed there. Few people went shopping for seeds and bulbs the day before New Year's.

Her stomach twisted at the thought of the evening ahead of her. New Year's Eve. It was supposed to be a time for looking back on the year with thanks, and for looking forward to the coming year with hope and expectation. She felt anything but.

Still, she would be there with bells on—for Reb. Regardless of whether they were to marry, she was still his friend and wanted to stand beside him and for this evening to be the kind of wonderful experience for him that he deserved.

But it would be the hardest thing she'd ever done to stand there with Griff, too, and say nothing. She'd wanted badly to tell him yesterday that she and Reb were no longer engaged, but she was honor-bound not to say anything.

Yet she knew Reb wouldn't mind if she told Griff. She'd elected not to, wanting instead for him to take that first step, to risk it all for love of her.

But they both had said nothing, would say nothing, would not speak, would not risk themselves. It'd be amusing if it weren't so sad.

Once ensconced behind the lawn mowers, Julia asked, "What's troubling you, Kelly? Did something happen with Jace?"

The little girl nodded miserably. "At church on Christmas. I waited afterward just so I could walk out with him. I wanted to give him the Christmas present I bought him. I thought and thought for weeks what I'd get him, and then I saw it last week when I went with my daddy to the tack and feed store."

She glanced up at Julia, her heart in her eyes. "I got him a brand-new catch rope— top of the line, too."

Julia stifled a gasp. "Ropes like that cost a lot, Kelly. Where'd you get the kind of money for a catch rope?"

"I—I had some savings," she said defiantly. "My grandmas always send me money along with birthday presents, and I've been saving my 'lowance for a long time."

She lowered her eyes. "Mama and Daddy don't know I took that money and spent it. And then Jace didn't want it! I went to give it to him, I even put a red bow on it, and he just looked at it! He wouldn't take it or nothing. So I ran away."

Her lower lip trembled. "Oh, Miss Sennett, I know he doesn't like me. I know it! Not the way I like him. I shouldn't've said anything!" Tears spilled down her cheeks. "How'm I gonna go back to school next week and see him every day? He won't ever want to talk to me again."

"Aw, honey." Julia dropped to her knees and engulfed the little girl in her arms, feeling Kelly's pain as if it were her own. And in a way it was—not exactly hers, but Griff's.

Griff who had said nothing of his love for her for so long, believing it best, doing it out of love for his other best friend. Yesterday's argument with him had been as painful as walking on hot coals. Was she wrong to have wanted him to speak, even without knowing the situation between herself and Reb, wrong to still want him to take that risk? She needed it from him.

But he needed something from her, as well—the risk of her heart loving him with completeness.

Why couldn't she give him that? Why? *That,* if anything, would ruin their friendship, for true friends didn't love conditionally any more than lovers did.

"Who knows why Jace didn't take your present," Julia told Kelly, her cheek pressed to the child's crown. "But don't punish yourself for taking the risk of putting your feelings for him out there."

She thought of Griff, and how he finally *had* spoken, even though it had been too late. "That's never a bad thing. And it doesn't change the fact that you're friends."

"Yes, it does!" Kelly said with a perceptivity beyond her years. "It changes it because he knows now!"

"Then you've got to be brave and honest and hold your head up high, and ask him for the same honesty. You deserve that from him. He doesn't hate you. Jace isn't that kind of boy. I know it in my heart."

But Kelly couldn't be consoled. And so Julia slid to the floor, her back against a stack of garden hoses, and held the little girl's broken heart against her own.

BRIDGEWATER HAD OUTDONE itself. The church hall, decorated within an inch of its life in bright red, white and blue streamers and balloons, looked as if it had never hosted anything so prosaic as a potluck, bake sale or bazaar. There was even a revolving disco ball hanging from the ceiling, and it scattered showers of white sparkles over the entire assemblage. There were games for the children in one corner, and the occasional whoop of excitement when a piñata had been well struck kept the noise level at a dull roar.

True to form, Alma Butters had appointed herself mistress of ceremonies, but her remarks were kept to a minimum by the C and W band, who kept serving up foot-stomping song after foot-stomping song.

From her post on the sidelines, Julia could see that Connor Brody seemed intent on keeping his fiancée breathless with laughter as he spun her around the dance floor. Lara's parents, Doo and Pauline, back from Phoenix for a few days, were cutting quite a rug, as well. They were egged on by Frannie and Andy, who seemed quite content to sit at a table covertly holding hands beneath it. The two couldn't quite seem to hide how happy they were.

The sight of the couples brought a lump to Julia's throat. She was so glad for them all—they'd each gone through so much to find happiness—and in a small corner of her heart Julia tried to believe that such happiness was at the end of her rainbow, too. She must not give up hope that it was.

There was no sign of Griff, however. She wondered if he'd changed his mind about coming. Could she blame him if he had?

"Julia! How nice to see you in a setting other than parent-teacher conferences!" said Addie Larrabie, looking as svelte on her husband's arm as if she'd never given birth to a girl barely two months ago, Julia thought admiringly.

"It's good to see you again," Julia said.

"I don't mind saying it feels good to get out!" she exclaimed, glancing around at the festive gathering with bright eyes. "Ever since the baby was born, I've felt as cooped up as a broody hen with a daily quota of eggs to lay. Not that I don't adore every minute with little Lorna!" she hastily added.

Deke, her husband, only laughed. "I know you do, darlin'. But it's been rough on you not to be out on the range riding the herd."

"Well, as far as the doctor's concerned, I

can start spending a little time in the saddle startin' next week. Daddy's said not to worry a bit about the baby. He'll take care of her real well. He's baby-sitting tonight, in fact—just the little one. Jace would've thrown a fit if we tried to leave him at home."

Julia's heart leapt to her throat as she glanced around just in time to see Jace himself approach Kelly.

"'Lo, Kelly," the boy said to her. He was such a handsome youngster, with dark hair and green-gold eyes just like his father's, that Julia could see how Kelly might be smitten.

"Hello, Jace," she said formally and just a little coldly, which made Julia worry that the girl might give in to her pride.

But then she said, "'fore I forget, Jace, I wanted to tell you…I didn't mean to make you feel, y'know, funny last week after church." She stopped, clearly mortified, then seemed to make herself go on, "When I tried to give you that catch rope, I mean. I hope you're not mad at me."

Jace's eyebrows screwed together in confusion. "'Course I'm not mad at you. I just couldn't take your present 'cause I didn't have one to give you back."

"I wasn't expecting one," the little girl

mumbled, gaze downcast and red-cheeked from embarrassment at having to explain her intent with an audience looking on. "That wasn't why I wanted to give you somethin' for Christmas. I wanted to 'cause…because you and me are friends."

"Well, 'Course we are," Jace said. "That's why I got you this."

And he thrust a package into her hands.

Though clearly surprised, Kelly took it, her hands shaking as she tore the Christmas wrapping away to reveal a small jewelry box. She tilted up its lid to reveal a delicate necklace with a silver heart.

"My mama helped me pick it out." Jace crammed his fists into his trouser pockets and shifted on his feet. "She said women any age like jewelry. It's not real silver," he apparently felt compelled to admit.

"It…it's beautiful," Kelly breathed.

Addie bent to whisper in her son's ear, "Help her put it on, Jace."

The boy dutifully took the chain and held it up as Kelly turned in a move of premature sophistication so that Jace could fasten it around her neck.

"Thank you, Jace," she said, again with that formality that held all the dignity of a queen.

The boy actually ducked his chin and scuffed the floor with the toe of his boot in a visual *Aw, shucks.* "You're welcome, Kelly."

Above their heads, the adults smiled indulgently.

Then Jace glanced over at the buffet table with barely disguised longing. "Wouldja like some cherry pie?" he asked Kelly. "I helped my mama bake it, but she wouldn't let me have none till we got here."

Kelly giggled, back to being eight years old. "Okay!"

Julia looked after them fondly as they tore off. What dear, brave children! She was proud to be their teacher. Proud to be playing even a small part in helping them sort out the world and how they fit into it.

A burst of male laughter caught her attention. Gathered around the keg were a group of young cowboys who were obviously paying homage to the rodeo champion. Reb saw her looking his way and excused himself to come over.

"I didn't mean to pull you away from your adoring public," she teased.

"I was waitin' for ten minutes for you to finally glance over so's I'd have a reason to get out of that."

His gaze scanned the crowd as if to anticipate getting waylaid by another bunch of young waddies.

"So how're you doin'?" he asked under his breath.

"Fine. How about you?"

"Well, let's see—the whole town's turned out to give me a welcome fit for a conquerin' king. How could I not be on top of the world?" he quipped.

But she saw the pain flash through his eyes. Yes, they were still friends, but it would take time for the hurts to heal.

She took his hand, and he gave hers a grateful squeeze back without letting go.

Then, as if compelled by an unseen force, Julia turned from him. The crowd, which was thick as a swarm of locusts, parted all of a sudden, and she had a clear view of the entrance to the hall. And there, at the door, stood Griff.

He wore black pants again, with a white Western shirt that stood out like a beacon among the holiday greens and reds and golds of the other partygoers. His wavy hair, dark as the night sky, fell over his forehead and kept him from appearing too reserved.

Julia drank in the sight of him as if she hadn't seen him in a score of years, the ache of her love for him like the hitched gait of his that would remain a constant reminder of the pain and loss he bore.

And with a sinking heart she knew it would always be this way. Whatever hurts she and Griff bore, they wouldn't be as quickly or as easily healed, if ever, as those she shared with Reb.

Then her gaze shifted to Michele, who linked her arm in his, her dress a profusion of violet-blue spangles that Julia recognized as being the exact shade as Griff's eyes. She wondered if Michele had planned it that way. Julia hoped so; to have it be accidental seemed too definite a sign—of what, she wasn't sure.

"Julia."

She turned distractedly to find Reb looking at her with a mixture of compassion and regret.

"Have you told Griff we're not gettin' married?" he asked gently.

She shook her head.

He inclined his head in Griff's and Michele's direction. "You might want to, and right quick, from the looks of things."

"This is your night, Reb," she said, avoiding addressing his implication. "I'd never do anything to spoil it."

"I think this situation comes under the heading of extenuating circumstances, though, don't you?" he said mildly.

Across the room, Michele smiled up at Griff as she brushed something off his shoulder. He smiled back, and it was the Griff he hadn't been with her for what seemed an age.

"Oh, Reb! It's more than that," Julia choked. "I think Griff and I are different from you. You go after what you want. Us—we seem, for whatever reason, to hold back, especially when it counts the most."

He made a dismissing *pffft* with his lips. "Sorry, Jules, but I find that hard to believe. Look at the way you went to work with those children in Central America, knowing it would be hard as anything could be."

"But that wasn't difficult, not really," she protested. "I mean, when you're dealing with what matters most in the world, you *want* to take those risks. It's worth it, because that's when you feel you're most alive."

A thought struck her. "I told Griff exactly that, not too long ago."

"And what did he say?"

"He said it was hard to stay in that state of

being, hard to get to, because so many of our doubts and fears get in the way." She concentrated, trying to remember the rest. "But he said he believes that we're meant to try, because that's what makes life worth living."

Reb actually laughed. "He's right, you know. In fact, I gotta tell you, Jules, Griff is the poster boy for riskin' it all."

"He is?" Griff had always seemed to her to take the most cautious road, to keep risks to a minimum.

"Of course," Reb answered. "Hell, didn't he jump in front of a rip-snortin' bull for love of his best friend? For love of you? That's not a man who's faint of heart, believe me."

She stared at him, barely seeing his face as she found herself at fifteen years old again and sitting on the fence watching Griff run straight for Reb and that bull. Run straight into danger. Yes, Griff had taken the hit for Reb that terrible day, and would do it again for his friend in an instant.

But he'd done it for her, too. She'd asked him to stop Reb, to save him. And he'd do *that* again, risk his life again so that he could live up to her faith in him, in an instant.

Because he loved her.

The breath left her lungs as Julia came back

to the present. Her hand shook as she lifted it to brush a lock of hair from her cheek.

"I never thought of it that way," she said. Why, just yesterday she had practically accused Griff of never making a stand, never taking a risk!

Her gaze jerked to Reb's, stricken. "Oh, how could I have been so blind?"

"You weren't blind—just scared. Scared for him."

It was all too much to take in. "I don't understand, though, Reb. If you knew he loved me, why did you ask me out—ask me to marry you?"

"Because I loved you, too." He dropped his chin, his face a mask of suppressed pain. "I'm not proud to admit it, but I was jealous, more than anything, at being left out. The two of you had a special bond I didn't share in. That's what made me act like such a fool and try to impress you by hopping into the corral with that bull."

His gaze grew distant, as if he also had journeyed back to the moment of Griff's accident. "Believe me, I'd give anything to change that day. I went through such agonies of guilt over almost gettin' my best friend killed competing for your attention, that I made it my personal mission to make good on having been so reckless. I loved riding the broncs, but after Griff's accident I set my sights on becoming the top bull rider in the world."

His eyes cleared and came back around to her. "In the instant I hit that mark, though, I knew I hadn't done it for myself, or even for you. I did it for Griff."

"I—I don't know what to say, Reb," Julia breathed. Once again it struck her how much had resided within her heart for years that she hadn't realized—most of all that she had all the answers she sought. "I didn't know."

"I didn't know myself." Reb took a deep breath. "That's the thing, Julia. Griff had the strength of character to stand aside while the woman he loved planned to marry and make a life with his best friend. So it seems like I ought to be able to do the same, you know?"

She turned, locating Griff again. He held two Dixie cups of beer in his hands as he made his way through the crowd. She was suddenly anxious that she tell him of her revelation and that *she* would not hold back any longer. Except—

"He's with Michele right now," she said, her heart twisting with disappointment as she saw him hand his date a cup, saw Michele thank him with another of her hold-nothing-back smiles.

The terrible possibility that it was already too late reared its ugly head.

"Well, it's up to you when you talk to Griff, if you think one more day won't make a difference," Reb told her. "But don't let me hold you back."

And she knew suddenly, though, that a single moment in time *could* make a difference. Of that she had ample evidence. That was why she needed to seize the moment. Seize the day.

For there truly *was* nothing holding her back—except her own fears.

"Thank you, Reb," Julia said, tiptoeing to kiss his cheek. "For everything."

"Don't mention it, darlin'," he said, his voice rough. "Now go get your cowboy."

Julia squared her shoulders, never feeling as sure of her purpose as then. Just as she started through the gathering toward Griff, though, Alma Butters's voice rang out from the P.A. system.

"Well, everyone, I see that the best man's arrived, so let's get on with the program!"

Her steel-gray beehive hairdo wobbled like a teetering skyscraper as she gestured to Reb.

"Come on up here, Rayburn," she ordered. "You know we won't be satisfied till we get a speech out of you—and a definite date when you and your bride-to-be are finally getting hitched!"

GRIFF HAD OFTEN wondered why he'd been tested throughout his life, and now he knew. It was so he would have the strength to make it through this evening.

He watched, his stomach a mass of knots, as Reb climbed almost reluctantly the steps to the stage. At first he didn't see Julia among the people who drifted closer to the front of the room. Then he spied the crown of her golden hair and wondered how on earth he could have missed her.

She was all in winter-white, like the bride she'd just been called, her dress a long-sleeved shimmery satin that clung to her gentle curves.

As if by design, she turned then, and their gazes unerringly met and clung, and it seemed as if a thousand possibilities existed in her eyes—but only for this moment.

And somehow in that instant it was like falling in love with her all over again: the heart palpitations, the topsy-turvy motion of his stomach, the singing of his heart.

The uncertainty...and the certainty that to never look into those hazel eyes—like stars they were—with the kind of love he was experiencing now was utterly inconceivable.

"Y'all want a speech, huh?" Reb said, distracting Griff.

His best friend stood on the stage, features shaded by his hat brim and one hip shot as he rubbed his chin.

The crowd hooted and hollered their answer.

"Well, I can't say as I'm much at talkin'," he continued. "But I guess if there's a better reason than this one, I don't know it. That's because I wouldn't be up here tonight bein' honored by all you fine folk if it weren't for a few people in my life who were always there for me and always believed in me."

He tipped his hat back with the edge of his index finger, his gaze making its way around the hall. "Two of those people are my parents, of course—Sue and Gary Farley. Mom, Dad, I love you."

Applause broke out as Griff spotted Reb's parents standing to one side. Tears streamed down Sue's face. Gary looked so proud a few

buttons seemed in peril of bursting off his
shirt.

"Now, if a person's got any luck in this
life," Reb went on, "he'll have maybe one
real, true friend who'll stand by him all his
life. Well, I don't know what I did to deserve
it, but I've got two such friends—Julia Sennett and Griff Corbin. I can truthfully say
there was never a time when the two of them
weren't behind me one hundred percent."

The roar was deafening. Griff wondered
if someone could get a spontaneous ulcer as
his stomach turned over on itself. If Reb only
knew…

"Julia!" Alma shaded her eyes against the
bright spotlight that had been rented especially for tonight. "Julia, come on up here
and join your fee-an-say so we can toast the
happy couple."

Griff tensed as he saw Julia demur before
finally allowing herself to be pulled onstage
next to Reb. She looked about as substantial
as a snowflake up there, her face as pale as
her dress.

Reb held out his hand to her, and she took
it and held on. The knot in Griff's stomach
gave another wicked twist.

Alma swished to the side of the stage,

where she retrieved two champagne flutes from Reb's mother. She handed them to Reb and Julia, then held her own cup of cider aloft. "Here's to our rodeo champion and the gal he'll marry!"

Around him, Griff felt rather than saw people lift whatever libation they had in their hands in a rowdy toast.

Alma took a healthy swig then set her hand on her hip as she turned a gimlet eye on the couple on the stage. "I told myself I wasn't goin' to let y'all get away tonight without announcin' your weddin' date. So come on, we all want to know, when're you two tyin' that knot?"

Reb looked at Julia. Julia looked at Reb. But neither said a word, and the moment dragged out not in anticipation but in awkwardness.

Griff felt rooted to the floor. What would either of them say once they began?

Alma huffed. "Well, someone better speak up here pretty darn quick, if there's to be a weddin' at all!"

Her words sounded like a church bell ringing in Griff's ears. Bits and snatches of phrases reverberated in his brain as if he stood in the very bell tower above them right now. ...*It couldn't be the same, but it could be different, something more...but I'd be a fool not to take the risk.*

It was more than he could bear. He had to do it: speak—or forever hold his peace. And he didn't think he'd been tested all his life for *that,* not when the fact was he couldn't hold back, not anymore.

He turned to the woman at his side. "I'm sorry, Michele."

She glanced up at him, puzzled. "Sorry? For what?"

He was agonizingly aware that a murmur had started to filter through the crowd at Reb's and Julia's continued silence. "I—I don't know you very well, but I already know you're an honest woman who'd want any man you were with to be honest with you."

"Honest about what?" she asked.

"I don't know any other way to say this. I'm in love with Julia, and I've got to let her know it, right now if not sooner."

"You mean, your friend Julia?" Michele said disbelievingly.

"Yes—but she's more than a friend. And I'm not going to let anything stand in the way of my love for her, not any longer. Like her being engaged to my best friend."

Michele shook her head. "She loves Reb, though, doesn't she? Or why would she be engaged to him?"

"Sure, but she loves me, too. It's complicated." He gave her a peck on the cheek. "Look, I'll give you a ride home after I tell her, if you want to leave. Or if you're not too thrilled about goin' anywhere with me, I'll arrange to find you a ride home. Right now, though, I've got something to do."

Griff pivoted. "Wait!" he called over the noise of the crowd. "I want to say something!"

And he began to make his way to the stage.

"Griff! Yes, come on up here with your best friends," Alma said.

The murmur of the crowd grew as he walked, people moving aside, their faces alight with curiosity. Never was he more aware of his hitched gait as then. Never was he more aware of the beating of his heart. Never did he feel so scared—or so alive.

Finally he stood in front of the stage. Both Reb and Julia peered down at him, but Griff could detect no ill will in either of their gazes. No, these two were his best friends. They would want only the best for him, as he so wanted the best for them.

"Reb, Julia." He got the names out only

after a few false starts. "Y'all know me as well as anyone on earth. You know my every fault, every foible, just as I know yours. I've always been the cautious one in the group, the one who asked questions first and acted later. And I have to say that's what made our friendship all work. But now...now something's come up where I've got to take action—and let the chips fall where they may."

He looked at Julia then, his heart in his eyes. "I love you, Julia. I can't give you up to marry my best friend without you both knowin' that. I know I'm risking losing the two of you as friends. But I have to speak. And to ask you, Julia, that if you want me, too, to take the risk of loving me."

Her hand covered her mouth, but whether in dismay or joy or shock, Griff couldn't tell. He had to go on, though.

"Y'see, I can't go on not taking risks, because to live is to risk. To love is to risk. And I do love you, Julia. Nothing can destroy the friendship between us—" he glanced at Reb, whose face told him nothing "—between all *three* of us. Nothing. That doesn't mean that our relationship won't change. By definition it will. But to change is to grow stronger, when there's love involved."

The hall was dead quiet, with the kind of pall reserved for moments of great awe or great horror—or of great volatility, such as the instant after a spark strikes in a firecracker factory—making Griff wonder which way the situation would go. And if he'd misspoken.

Then Julia turned to Reb—and nodded once. He stepped to the edge of the stage—and extended his hand to his friend.

Relief washing over him in a ten-foot-high wave, Griff took it, and Reb gave a mighty yank that helped Griff boost himself onstage in a single bound.

Hands still clasped, the two men looked into each other's eyes, and Griff saw understanding. And love—the love of his best friend that he had been sorely afraid he would never experience again.

Grinning at each other, Griff and Reb shook hands firmly. Then, in a gesture that Griff could barely believe, Reb joined his hand with Julia's. Griff's gaze met hers in question, and he saw there, too, the answer to his questions as well as to every unasked, unspoken concern he'd ever felt.

Her eyes shone with her love for him—as

her best friend, to be sure, but also as the man she wanted to spend the rest of her life with.

Reb gave a nod as his own hand clasped around theirs, supporting the bond between them.

"Y'all want to know when the wedding is?" he asked the crowd. "I'd say it can't be a moment too soon—not for these two. I think they've been waiting all their lives to marry, don't you?"

He glanced at Griff, who whispered a husky "I do." Then at Julia, whose murmured "I do" was like music.

"It's settled, then," Reb declared. "Far be it from me to stand in the way of my best friends' wedding!"

THE APPLAUSE AND cheering made Julia's head ache. But it felt good. How could it not?

Parents—hers, Griff's and Reb's—poured onto the stage, dispensing hugs and kisses like stumping politicians.

The first to find her was Reb's mother, whose hug was fierce and hard.

"You're not angry with me, Sue?" Julia asked tremulously. She couldn't bear to hurt either her or Gary.

"Hush, dear, I couldn't be mad at you if

they made it a law," Sue said. "You're like a daughter to me, just as Griff's like a son. Besides, Reb's right. I think we always knew you and Griff were meant to be together. In fact, I'd say this marriage's been planned since you were born."

Griff's mother had tears of wonder in her eyes. "Yes! When I met your mother, Julia, it was when we both stood looking at you and Griff in the nursery. Your hair was so blond—almost white—and Griff's was so dark and wavy, and I said to Mary Jo, 'Don't the two of them look like a little bride and groom?'"

"But then Reb's bassinet got put between," Sue chimed in. "I swear, the way you and Griff cried at that, Julia, you'd have thought the nurses were starvin' you both!"

"Oh, and do you remember what happened next?" Frannie asked her. "The two of them crying started Reb crying, he was just so un-happy at making them unhappy. Once the nurse moved him to the other side of Griff, though, he was happy as a clam."

"So," Julia said softly, "Fate knew what it was doing, after all. And so did we."

They all looked at her curiously.

"Hey, y'all, it's almost midnight!" someone in the crowd shouted.

Alma led the countdown to midnight, the band providing a drumroll. "Five…four…three…two…one! Happy New Year!"

Balloons in every color rained down from the ceiling. Streamers shot forth from fists like magic, and every child with a horn blew it for all it was worth.

Julia found herself engulfed in a hug from Reb's father, then his mother, then her own father, and on down the line to Reb, who held her tight for a brief moment before letting her go with a kiss on her cheek.

Then she turned, and there was Griff. He held out his hand, and she went to him—her best friend, her lover, her partner in life.

"Happy New Year, darlin'," he whispered just before he dipped his head to take her lips in a thoroughly thrilling, thoroughly branding kiss that left Julia's heart pounding and her knees weak.

But there was no way Griff would let her fall. No way he'd let her go, ever again.

"I can barely believe this is true." He breathed in a perfect echo of her thoughts, his eyes drinking in her every feature. Julia reveled in it.

"I've been such a fool," he said, his arms linked around her waist. "Foolish to think that the love we feel for each other could ever end."

"You're not foolish," Julia admonished gently. "What's the saying? Something like, 'Fools rush in where angels fear to tread'? I'd say we've both done our share of hanging back out of fear."

"Maybe." His violet-blue eyes grew wicked then. "Except I'm no angel."

And he melded his lips to hers again in a fiery kiss that Julia returned with all her heart.

He was right, of course. It *had* been entirely foolish to fear even for a moment that their love wasn't meant to be.

For, like his kiss, it could only go on and on and on....

* * * * *

YES! Please send me the *Cowboy at Heart* collection in Larger Print. This collection begins with 3 FREE books and 2 FREE gifts in the first shipment, and more free gifts will follow! My books will arrive in 8 monthly shipments until I have the entire 51-book *Cowboy at Heart* collection. I will receive 2 or 3 FREE books in each shipment and I will pay just $4.99 U.S./ $5.89 CDN. for each of the other four books in each shipment, plus $2.99 for shipping and handling.* If I decide to keep the entire collection, I'll have paid for only 32 books because 19 books are FREE! I understand that by accepting the 3 free books and gifts places me under no obligation to buy anything. I can always return a shipment and cancel at any time. My free books and gifts are mine to keep no matter what I decide.

256 HCN 0807   456 HCN 0807

Name	(PLEASE PRINT)	

Address		Apt. #

City	State/Prov.	Zip/Postal Code

Signature (if under 18, a parent or guardian must sign)

Mail to the **Harlequin®** Reader Service:
IN U.S.A.: P.O. Box 1867, Buffalo, NY 14240-1867
IN CANADA: P.O. Box 609, Fort Erie, Ontario L2A 5X3

* Terms and prices subject to change without notice. Prices do not include applicable taxes. Sales tax applicable in N.Y. Canadian residents will be charged applicable taxes. This offer is limited to one order per household. All orders subject to approval. Credit or debit balances in a customer's account(s) may be offset by any other outstanding balance owed by or to the customer. Please allow 4 to 6 weeks for delivery. Offer available while quantities last. Offer not available to Quebec residents.

Your Privacy—The Harlequin® Reader Service is committed to protecting your privacy. Our Privacy Policy is available online at www.ReaderService.com or upon request from the Harlequin Reader Service.

We make a portion of our mailing list available to reputable third parties that offer products we believe may interest you. If you prefer that we not exchange your name with third parties, or if you wish to clarify or modify your communication preferences, please visit us at www.ReaderService.com/consumerschoice or write to us at Harlequin Reader Service Preference Service, P.O. Box 9062, Buffalo, NY 14269. Include your complete name and address.

CAHBPA13B

ReaderService.com

Manage your account online!
- Review your order history
- Manage your payments
- Update your address

*We've designed
the Harlequin® Reader Service
website just for you.*

Enjoy all the features!
- Reader excerpts from any series
- Respond to mailings and special monthly offers
- Discover new series available to you
- Browse the Bonus Bucks catalog
- Share your feedback

Visit us at:
ReaderService.com

RS13

REQUEST YOUR FREE BOOKS!
2 FREE WHOLESOME ROMANCE NOVELS IN LARGER PRINT
PLUS 2 FREE MYSTERY GIFTS

⚜⚜⚜⚜⚜⚜⚜⚜⚜⚜⚜⚜⚜⚜⚜⚜⚜⚜⚜⚜⚜⚜

H E A R T W A R M I N G™

Wholesome, tender romances

YES! Please send me 2 FREE Harlequin® Heartwarming Larger-Print novels and my 2 FREE mystery gifts (gifts worth about $10). After receiving them, if I don't wish to receive any more books, I can return the shipping statement marked "cancel." If I don't cancel, I will receive 4 brand-new larger-print novels every month and be billed just $4.99 per book in the U.S. or $5.74 per book in Canada. That's a savings of at least 23% off the cover price. It's quite a bargain! Shipping and handling is just 50¢ per book in the U.S. and 75¢ per book in Canada.* I understand that accepting the 2 free books and gifts places me under no obligation to buy anything. I can always return a shipment and cancel at any time. Even if I never buy another book, the two free books and gifts are mine to keep forever.

161/361 IDN F47N

Name	(PLEASE PRINT)	
Address		Apt. #
City	State/Prov.	Zip/Postal Code

Signature (if under 18, a parent or guardian must sign)

Mail to the **Harlequin® Reader Service:**
IN U.S.A.: P.O. Box 1867, Buffalo, NY 14240-1867
IN CANADA: P.O. Box 609, Fort Erie, Ontario L2A 5X3

* Terms and prices subject to change without notice. Prices do not include applicable taxes. Sales tax applicable in N.Y. Canadian residents will be charged applicable taxes. Offer not valid in Quebec. This offer is limited to one order per household. Not valid for current subscribers to Harlequin Heartwarming larger-print books. All orders subject to credit approval. Credit or debit balances in a customer's account(s) may be offset by any other outstanding balance owed by or to the customer. Please allow 4 to 6 weeks for delivery. Offer available while quantities last.

Your Privacy—The Harlequin® Reader Service is committed to protecting your privacy. Our Privacy Policy is available online at www.ReaderService.com or upon request from the Harlequin Reader Service.

We make a portion of our mailing list available to reputable third parties that offer products we believe may interest you. If you prefer that we not exchange your name with third parties, or if you wish to clarify or modify your communication preferences, please visit us at www.ReaderService.com/consumerchoice or write to us at Harlequin Reader Service Preference Service, P.O. Box 9062, Buffalo, NY 14269. Include your complete name and address.

HWDIR13R